Maizon at Blue Hill

Also by Jacqueline Woodson

Maizon at Blue Hill

Jacqueline Woodson

Published by
Delacorte Press
Bantam Doubleday Dell Publishing Group, Inc.
666 Fifth Avenue
New York, New York 10103

Library of Congress Cataloging in Publication Data
Woodson, Jacqueline.
Maizon at Blue Hill : book two about Maizon and Margaret / Jacqueline Woodson.
p. cm.
Summary: After winning a scholarship to an academically challenging boarding school, Maizon finds herself one of only five blacks there and wonders if she will ever fit in. Sequel to "Last Summer with Maizon."
ISBN 0-385-30796-9
[1. Afro-Americans—Fiction. 2. Schools—Fiction. 3. Gifted children —Fiction.] I. Title.
PZ7.W868Mai 1992
[Fic]—dc20 91-44295 CIP AC

Manufactured in the United States of America

October 1992

10 9 8 7 6 5 4 3 2 1

BVG

For
Jillian Marie,
Samantha Nicole,
Isidora Milin Finkelstein,
and Avery Brooks

The author wishes to thank the MacDowell Colony for its support, Marjorie Snyder and the Women's Sports Foundation for information, Teresa Calabrese, Wendy Lamb, and Sue Scarfe for guidance, and Liza Voges and Linda Villarosa for having faith.

An extremely special thanks to the students at the George School in Newtown, Pennsylvania, who read parts of this in its scary early stages, and the students at Nathan Bishop Middle School in Providence, Rhode Island, who listened to *me* read parts of this in its scary early stages.

When I see birches bend to left and right
Across the lines of straighter darker trees,
I like to think some boy's been swinging them.
But swinging doesn't bend them down to stay
As ice-storms do.

—"Birches," Robert Frost

The higher you build your barriers
The taller I become. . . .
The farther you take my rights away
The faster I will run. . . .

The more you refuse to hear my voice
The louder I will sing. . . .
The more you refuse the things I need . . .
The more I want everything. . . .

There's something inside so strong
I know that I can make it. . . .

Labi Siffr

Maizon at Blue Hill

Chapter One

"Would you look at *this*?" Grandma said. We were sitting on the couch in the living room. Mr. Parsons, from the Blue Hill School, sat across from us, smiling.

"That's the hill the school was named for," he said, pointing toward the picture Grandma was looking at. I frowned at him and rolled my eyes. Did he think Grandma and me were bozos or something? The hill *was* blue—well, sort of. It looked like it was covered with moss and grass at the same time. Flowers, planted to spell out "Blue Hill School," grew around the edge of it.

"Isn't this beautiful, Maizon?" Grandma pushed the photograph toward me. There was a stack of them on her lap and we had been looking at them all morning. Mr. Parsons was full of pictures and pamphlets and information about Blue Hill. All I wanted was to stay right on Madison

Street with my best friend, Margaret, to go to P.S. 102 instead of some school in Connecticut.

I had plans for the fall. I was going to find out where our neighbor, Ms. Dell's, special powers came from and if there was a tiny, tiny chance that she might be planning on passing them on to me.

"You're going to love it, Maizon," Grandma said. Mr. Parsons smiled and nodded. *You don't even know me, man,* I wanted to say to him. *How would you know what I'm going to like?*

"It looks nice, Grandma," I said instead, because I knew all summer long Grandma had been bragging to people about me going away to Blue Hill.

"Are there other black girls there, Mr. Parsons?"

Mr. Parsons blinked. "Yes, Maizon. Of course there are other black girls."

"Then how come there aren't any in any of these pictures? We must have looked at a hundred of them. And how come there aren't any in this?" I waved the catalog at him.

"The catalog needs to be updated, Maizon," he said slowly. "We're working on doing that this year. Blue Hill is actually somewhat behind other schools, in a way." Mr. Parsons cleared his throat before continuing. "While we have small classes with caring teachers and some of the best athletic equipment, we're still working on being more inclusive—bringing in more minorities and students who financially wouldn't be able to have a boarding school experience if it weren't for scholarship. . . ."

I listened to him drone on for a while. I hated the word *minorities*. I mean, who decides who becomes a *minority*? Personally, I don't consider myself less than anyone. When Mr. Parsons got to the part in his speech about the great founders of Blue Hill, I tuned him out. It was a trick I had. I could make a person disappear just by not listening to him.

"I wish I could take the whole trip up there. . . ." Grandma was saying when I tuned back in.

"You can't, Grandma. Your legs." Grandma had been having trouble with her legs all summer. Even though the doctor said it was nothing to worry about, he had warned her that she shouldn't walk far distances and shouldn't take long rides. Blue Hill was three hours away by train. "And plus, you promised that if I went there, I could take the train up most of the way by myself. You *promised.*"

Grandma sighed and put up her hand. "I know, I know, Maizon. You're a big girl now. Don't worry. I won't go back on my word."

Mr. Parsons rose and Grandma handed him the stack of pictures. "The board was really impressed with your interview, Maizon," he said. "They think you'll be an asset to Blue Hill."

I nodded. It had been so long ago, I had nearly forgotten the day Grandma took me to Queens to meet with a group of teachers from Blue Hill. They seemed nice enough. Teachers were teachers. They were always asking you questions and then acting surprised because you knew the right answers. The Blue Hill people asked questions like all the others, opening their eyes wide when I answered them correctly, shaking their heads like they were disappointed in me when I didn't.

I got up and locked the door behind Mr. Parsons, then came back to sit beside Grandma. She was knitting me a red sweater. The collar would be black. Those were my favorite colors together—black and red. If Blue Hill had black-and-red uniforms, I'd be there in a quick minute. But seventh graders—or lower school freshmen, as Mr. Parsons called them—had to wear green-and-black plaid blazers with white blouses and green skirts. I hated green.

Grandma rested her knitting in her lap and pulled me closer to her. "Maizon," she said softly, "I know you think I'm evil for sending you away . . ."

I swallowed. Evil is not the word I would have used.

"But," Grandma continued, "you have to understand that going away is going to make you a different person."

"I don't want to be differ—"

"Shush, Maizon," Grandma said softly. "Let me explain. Everybody wants a safe place. For me it was Colorado on the reservation. But I knew if I wanted to grow I had to leave. Madison Street is your safe place. But if you stay here too long, you'll begin to think that this is all there is to life. I want you to see that there is more, that there are other people who have lives that are different from lives you know here. I want you to experience difference, Maizon. You were the only girl in Brooklyn to pass the exam for Blue Hill. The *only* one. Don't you understand what that means? It means this is a chance for you to learn beyond the boundaries of Brooklyn. Outside of New York City. There is more than this, Maizon. There's a whole *world.* You need to see that. And the only way to do so is to leave. This is a beginning for you. I think you're ready."

Beyond the boundaries of Brooklyn. Margaret and I had never even stepped a foot outside of Brooklyn. We had made a promise to see Manhattan together when we saw it for the first time. Margaret and I had made lots of promises to each other. We wanted to be best friends . . . always.

"Anybody could have passed that stupid test, Grandma. They didn't even let Margaret take it.

She would've passed and then at least me and her could still be together. . . ."

"You'll be together, Maizon. You and Margaret will always be together. Right here." She pressed her finger to my chest. "That's what makes best friends. It's not whether or not you live on the same block or go to the same school, but how you feel about each other in your hearts."

I felt a lump rising in the back of my throat and swallowed. "What if we change, Grandma? What if I come home and Margaret's not my best friend anymore? Then I won't have anybody."

Grandma shook my shoulders and grinned. "What about this old lady, Maizon?"

I looked up at Grandma. We had been together since I was a baby. Leaving her was too hard even to think about. "You're in my heart, Grandma."

Grandma smiled, picking up her needles again and snapping them together so quickly they nearly blurred. "Maizon, Maizon, Maizon . . ." she said softly. "What *am* I going to do with you?"

"Well, you could *not* send me to Blue Hill. That would be a start."

"And then what? You're too smart for the schools here in Brooklyn."

"What if I just skipped a grade, Grandma? Then I'd be okay."

Grandma frowned. "I want you to learn with children your own age, Maizon. I don't want you to grow up before you need to."

"I *won't* grow up before I need to, Grandma. Promise! I'll just go to class and do my work. Then I'll come home and be with Margaret and Ms. Dell and Hattie and Li'l Jay. That's all."

"You'll start wanting to do the things your classmates will be doing. Maybe they'll be able to stay up an hour later than you do. Then you'll want to stay up late because they'll make fun of you if they know your bedtime. Then you'll want to go out with them and stay out late. It won't be good."

"But if I'm smart like the older kids then why can't I go to school with them and do the things they do?" I pressed my hands together in my lap to keep from getting mad. Grandma was stubborn. She said that's where I got it from.

"You grow up faster than you need to, Maizon, and trust me, you'll be dragging your feet to slow your growing up down."

I got up and walked over to the window. Outside, the sun was yellow-orange against Grandma's shrubs. I leaned against the sill and pressed my hand to the glass.

Grandma had made me the shorts set I was wearing. The top was blue-and-red striped and the shorts were all blue with only a little bit of red around the pockets. At Blue Hill I wouldn't be able to wear shorts sets Grandma made me. I wouldn't be able to sit beside her on the couch and argue with her while she knitted. At Blue Hill, I knew, I wouldn't be able to do *anything*.

The lump was back in my throat again. I didn't swallow this time, and soon tears were pushing against the back of my eyes.

It had been decided.

Chapter Two

"Yo! Margaret!"

Margaret raised her window and stared down at me through the metal slats of her fire escape. "Shhh, Maizon. Li'l Jay's sleeping."

"Come outside," I whispered as loud as I could, because she lived on the sixth floor. That's why I had screamed in the first place.

"Come up," she whispered back. "Mama's still working. I gotta watch Li'l Jay until she gets home."

I pushed open the first door and waited for Margaret to buzz me through the second one, then raced up the five flights of stairs to her apartment.

"That's nice," Margaret said, pointing her chin toward my outfit.

I rolled my eyes and plopped down on the couch. "Three more days in civilian clothes," I mumbled. "Three stupid days. Seventy-two hours.

Four thousand three hundred and twenty minutes."

"Two hundred and fifty-nine thousand two hundred seconds," Margaret finished, sitting down beside me.

"Cheese and crackers, Margaret," I said, because that's what Grandma wanted me to say instead of saying "Jesus Christ." "That's not any time at all. Even God got *seven* days."

Margaret nodded. "And God wasn't even going away." She handed me a stick of gum and took one out of the pack for herself. "You learned how to make sounds yet, Maizon?"

I pressed the gum into my mouth and shook my head. "I haven't practiced."

"I heard this girl down the block. She was clicking her gum a mile a minute. Click, click, click. It was something."

"Somebody told me you had to have a cavity to click it."

"I heard you had to have a filling, but I have a filling on my left side," Margaret said, pointing to her left cheek. "I've been trying for a long time and still, nothing."

"Anyway, Grandma says that's impolite, Margaret."

"Hattie can do it. She does it with any kind of gum."

Hattie, Ms. Dell's nineteen-year-old daughter, wasn't exactly my favorite person in the world.

"Hattie's impolite."

"She's nice, Maizon."

"Margaret, you think everybody's nice."

A pitiful look moved across Margaret's face. I glared at her, mad that she always broke so easily. But when the look settled in her eyes, I was sorry. Her father had died this summer. I didn't want to make her hurt any more than she was already hurting. After all, we *were* best friends.

"Sorry," I mumbled, putting my arm around her shoulder. "I'm just all mixed-up inside."

Margaret looked down at her fingernails. After a moment, she started picking at the skin around her cuticle. I smacked her hand away gently. "Don't, Margaret. You'll get yourself all scarred up."

Margaret shrugged. "Everything's all settled now, isn't it, Maizon? You're truly, surely going away, right?"

"We sent my trunk today. Mr. Parsons was just at my house. He had more pictures to show Grandma."

"But you and her already looked at all those slides. And she met some of the teachers and everything. Why do they have to keep coming back with more stuff and more stuff and more stuff?"

"Because Grandma can't go up to Blue Hill. They want to make sure she understands about the school and everything. I guess they want her to feel like she's been there."

"Oh," Margaret said, staring down at her hands again.

"Plus, they want me to get kind of used to the idea of being away at a place like that."

"Schools are schools. It's still teaching and learning and doing a ton and a half of homework instead of being able to watch a good movie."

Margaret looked at me and crossed her eyes. I laughed. Then Margaret started laughing too. After a moment, we weren't even sure what we were laughing about. Sometimes it felt so good just to be together that we couldn't help but giggle and act silly. Even if people stared at us and frowned. We didn't care.

I stopped laughing and leaned back against the couch.

"Here," Margaret said, handing me a small throw pillow, which I stuffed behind my head.

"I'm all crazy mixed-up inside," I said again, only whispering this time.

Margaret moved toward me, bringing her knees up and leaning her chin on them. "Because you're going away?"

I shrugged, pressing my palm against my mouth the way I do when I'm thinking. "It's more, though. It's going away, but it's more too."

"Like what?"

"Like, you remember how we used to sit under the tree when we were little and talk about the things we wanted to be?"

Margaret nodded. "*Little,* Maizon? We did that a month ago."

"It seems longer than that to me."

"I wanted to be a lawyer and a doctor and a writer."

"And I wanted to be a lawyer and a movie director and a writer."

"We could still be all those things. That's not going to change any."

"But those are the things I wanted to be *here,* on Madison Street. I might want to be somebody a whole lot different when I go away."

"Why?"

"Because there won't be a Ms. Dell at Blue Hill or you or Grandma or Junior—I mean, Li'l Jay—or Hattie. There won't be any of the people from this block. And those are all the people who have always been around me, saying *Do it, Maizon! Do it!* Now they're all singing a different song. They're all saying *Go to Blue Hill, Maizon!*"

"But that's them showing you the way to be who you want to be."

I looked at Margaret, all of sudden wanting to cry. Her hair was pulled back away from her face and braided down the back of her neck the way it usually was and her skin was the same caramel brown it had always been. She was right there in front of me—not even half a foot away. But even as we sat there talking, something was already moving in between us. We were slipping away from each other. It was like we had begun to speak different languages.

"You know how you hear a song, Margaret," I said, "and it could be about the dumbest thing, but when you hear it, something clicks inside of you and all of a sudden you want to cry?"

Margaret nodded.

"That's what this moment feels like to me."

"I'm feeling kind of choky, too, Maizon. But I don't really know why. I'm going to write you all the time."

"And I'm going to write you back. All the time. Maybe *two* letters a day."

Margaret shook her head. "You won't have time to do all that writing. You better think about doing a little studying, girl. Blue Hill is going to teach circles around your head."

"Shoot," I said, waving my hand. "That dumb school isn't *even* ready for me."

Margaret looked up at me and raised her eyebrows. But she didn't say anything.

Chapter Three

"Eeny Meeny Miney Mo. Let's catch Li'l Jay by his toe. If he hollers, don't let him go. Eeny Meeny Miney Mo," Ms. Dell sang, pulling on Li'l Jay's toes. He squealed, wiggling his feet away from her. Margaret's brother, Li'l Jay, would be sixteen months soon and with me and Margaret helping, he could walk almost anywhere.

We were sitting on Margaret's stoop, because it was too hot to stay upstairs. Ms. Dell and Hattie had joined us, folding out lawn chairs at the top of the stoop. They lived right downstairs from Margaret and loved our company. At least, that's what I heard Ms. Dell telling Grandma a while back. Margaret and I sat at their feet, on the top step. The stoop was hard and warm underneath me. A lawn chair of my own would have been nice.

"You got any more soda?" I asked Margaret, tipping her glass to my mouth. It was as empty as my own.

The block was noisy as usual with kids running up and down, darting between cars and hiding behind rows of garbage cans. Margaret and I were too cool to be bothered with silly neighborhood kids. But as I watched them round everybody up for a game of kick the can, I thought maybe I should join them, just one last time, since my days on Madison Street were numbered.

"Sing, Maizon," Margaret said, yanking my arm. "You have a good voice." Then she turned back toward Ms. Dell and Hattie, and started it up again. "Let's go. A let's go . . . A let's go . . . Eeny Meeny Miney Mo. Catch that baby by his toes . . ." Margaret sang at the top of her lungs.

"That's a dumb song," I said.

Ms. Dell cut her blue eyes at me. In the near-darkness, they looked even stranger against her dark skin. "Humph," she said. Then she gave Li'l Jay a shake and stood him on her lap. "Look at this baby's pretty little legs," she cooed.

"I've seen better legs on a table," I said.

Ms. Dell looked over at me again, then over at her daughter, Hattie, who was working the hem of a dress as she sang. Hattie would be twenty in December and Ms. Dell had told Grandma that Hattie couldn't move out of her teenage years fast enough. I knew what she meant. Hattie was downright evil sometimes. And besides that, she didn't like me much.

"Up with it, already, Maizon," Hattie said,

moving the dress across her lap and picking up the stitch again. The skirt was white, that kind of stretchy material Grandma didn't allow me to wear because she said I was too young to be trying to show off curves I didn't even have yet. The minute I got a curve, I was going to use my money to buy a dress like Hattie's. "What's nipping your nerves and making you so evil tonight?"

"She's got the Blue Hill blues," Margaret said.

Sometimes I wondered if somebody had passed Hattie over in the brain department. "And I sure don't feel like hearing anybody's bad singing tonight," I said.

Ms. Dell reared back in her chair like she had seen something scary. "You *are* evil."

"I wish," I said, holding up a finger. "I wish there was just *one* person on this crowded stoop who could understand what's going on inside my head. Just one. I'm not asking for a hundred people, I not even asking for fifty or ten. Just one person."

"I understand, Maizon," Margaret said. "I'm your best friend. So of course I understand."

"And Maizon," Ms. Dell said, "you *know* I understand."

"That's different, Ms. Dell. You have special powers." Ms. Dell had been born with the gift of clairvoyance. She could look right into a person's head and know everything that was going on there. Some people were scared of her. Not me and Margaret though. There wasn't much we wouldn't give to have her powers. I folded my arms across my chest and glared out into the street. The streetlights flickered on, casting a yellow glow out over the block. "Eavesdropping right inside a person's brain doesn't count."

"Well, don't expect *me* to understand you, Maizon," Hattie declared.

"Don't worry," I said. "I don't."

If anyone had asked, I'm sure neither of us could have said what it was we didn't like about the other. Ms. Dell said we were too much alike. She had a hard time understanding how we could like ourselves, let alone each other. "You're both so hateful at times," she'd said. Hattie once said I thought I was cute and I'd said back, "I think, therefore I am," which she thought was a smart aleck remark. For a teenager she didn't have much of a sense of humor. Too bad she was pretty. It's kind of a waste.

"Don't you two get started," Ms. Dell warned, shifting Li'l Jay on her lap. "Now, Maizon, I know you're all full of confusions about this school. But don't worry your pretty head over anything. I'll be with you."

"That's what everybody says, Ms. Dell. 'I'll be with you.' 'I'll be with you.' But when I get up to that school, it's going to be me. Maizon Singh. A-L-O-N-E."

"Never," Ms. Dell said softly.

"What?" I thought I hadn't heard her right.

Ms. Dell's brows moved in toward each other, sending the lines above them deeper into her forehead. "I said 'never.' If you live to be a hundred and seventy-five, Maizon Singh, and you, too, Margaret, and even you, Li'l Jay, you'll never be alone. You understand that?"

Margaret and I shook our heads quickly. I didn't believe it or understand it but I wasn't about to dispute Ms. Dell's word. Even Li'l Jay moved his head up and down when he saw us doing it.

Ms. Dell leaned back in her chair. "That's all I have to say."

"Eeny Meeny Miney Mo . . ." Hattie began. "Let's catch Maizon by her toe. If she hollers, don't let her go. Eeny Meeny Miney Mo . . ."

I felt a warm drop and looked up at the sky. There was no moon in sight. In a second, I felt another drop.

"See, Hattie," I said. "Your bad singing is making it rain."

Chapter Four

The M train moved slowly over the Williamsburg Bridge. Below us, the East River rippled and danced blue-gray like it was putting on a show for someone. Margaret had given me the window seat, since this would be my last ride on the M train for a long time. Across from us, Margaret's mother, Mrs. Tory, sat beside Grandma. Grandma was going to ride with me out of New York City. Then she would take a train back from Stamford. Blue Hill was a long way away. I drummed my fingers against the windowpane. My stomach felt like someone had tied it into a hundred knots and the knots were growing and growing.

At Penn Station the conductor called my train twice before I turned to Margaret. "I guess I gotta go," I said softly. "I'll write you back, Margaret. Promise. Thanks for letting me keep the double-dutch trophy, even if it is only second place." We hugged for a long time.

"I'm scared, Margaret," I whispered.

"Don't be," Margaret said.

Mrs. Tory bent down and hugged me. "Be good," she called as Grandma and I made our way toward the train. I couldn't look back. I couldn't stand to see them growing smaller and smaller and farther away from me. When I finally looked back, Margaret and Mrs. Tory were out of sight. I wanted to call to Margaret and tell her this was our first trip to Manhattan, the trip we had planned since we were little. I wanted her to reappear all of a sudden and yell, "Maizon, we did it! We finally got to the other side of the bridge!"

I must have slowed down some, because the next thing I knew, Grandma was taking my hand and leading me onto the train. My vision was blurred. A hundred thoughts were running through my head all at once. What if Mr. Parsons had lied? What if there were no other black girls there after all? What if I never saw Margaret again? Or Madison Street?

Grandma settled into the seat beside me, just as the train began to roll forward.

"This will be a nice ride for you, Maizon. You can watch yourself leaving the city behind."

I leaned on my hand and stared out the window. Tall gray buildings moved slowly past us. I had never thought about this particular ride. It was strange. People were always moving around, figuring ways of getting from one place to another. Every day they piled into Grand Central Station, then piled out again. Every day they got onto planes and climbed aboard buses and left somebody behind somewhere. Even while I was sitting there, somebody was kissing the person they loved good-bye somewhere and making all kinds of promises to write or call. I had two letters from Margaret stuffed in my knapsack with the double-dutch trophy we had won last summer. I had portions of our friendship with me—stuff that Margaret trusted me with. Maybe this was enough for now.

The gray buildings blurred into patches of green. It was cloudy outside and hot.

Grandma pulled me to her and I buried my head in her shoulder. "You'll be a different person from all of this, Maizon," she said, as though she were reading my mind. "I love you now. I'll love you later. Remember that."

I nodded.

"We're all going to miss you. Madison Street won't be the same, you know."

I nodded again and Grandma took my chin in her hands and pulled my face toward her. Tiny wrinkles crept away from the sides of her eyes when she smiled. "I'm so proud of you. If your mother were alive, she'd be proud too."

"You think my father would be proud,

Grandma?" My father had left me with Grandma when I was a baby. I knew it was because he was sad that Mama had died giving birth to me. Maybe he figured I would be too much trouble to raise. Grandma said I was no trouble at all.

"Your father would be proud. Very proud."

"I wish I knew where he went, Grandma. I wish I could just see him and say, 'Hi, Dad. Look how great I turned out to be. Okay. You can go away now.' "

Grandma laughed. My mother was her only daughter. Sometimes she hated my father for leaving, but she tried not to show it in front of me.

"I'm glad you kept me, Grandma. Thank you."

Grandma clucked her tongue. "We're two peas in a pod, Maizon. You just remember that. It was fate that brought us to each other—"

"But love that will keep us together," I finished.

Later, when the conductor announced Stamford, Grandma moved slowly to her feet.

"Hold on, Grandma. Wait till the train stops."

"I have to get a head start, Maizon. When you get to be my age, no one waits for you anymore."

"They better wait," I said, walking with Grandma to the front of the car. "You're my grandmother. So they better good and wait."

Grandma laughed, turning to me at the door.

"Here," she said, pressing bills into my hand. "For anything you might need."

"Like what? They feed you there and everything."

"Something unexpected might come up, Maizon. You have to be ready."

I nodded and Grandma leaned in to kiss me on the forehead. I knew what she meant, because we had a talk before I left. Grandma thought I might get my period at Blue Hill. I wasn't in any hurry to get it and neither was Margaret. If we didn't get it until we were sixteen, it wouldn't be a day too soon. I put the money in my pocket anyway.

"I'll miss you, Maizon," Grandma said. I hugged her until the doors opened. Even then, I didn't want to let her go.

"Good-bye, Grandma." I stood at the door and waved until the train started moving again. Then I kept waving until Grandma was out of sight. "I'll miss you so much."

Before sitting down again, I reached into my pocket. Two twenties and a ten.

Chapter Five

When the train pulled into the Canton station, it gave a loud sigh before jerking to a stop. Around me, people were hustling their bags from the overhead stand and moving slowly toward the door. I couldn't move. The clouds had faded away somewhere between New York and here and now the sun shone through honey-gold in the sky. I had never seen anything so beautiful.

A long time ago, Grandma told me the story of her first time in New York. She was twenty-five and had taken a bus from Colorado. It had taken seven days, with the bus stopping in different small towns throughout the night and people getting on and off around her. Grandma said she was the only one traveling by herself on the whole bus and that she felt the loneliness all through the days, driving through half-dead-looking towns and stopping at bus stops in places that looked like all there was to them was a bus stop. Then

Grandma leaned back on the sofa and pressed her hands together, and told me that she had to wait until the nighttime to cry because she didn't want people to know what kind of loneliness she was feeling. She said a bubble sat between her mouth and throat all day, and only when the moon was full up in the sky did she let it burst into tears.

"Canton. Last stop!" the conductor called. Outside, people moved quickly beneath my window. Far beyond them, green mountains loomed up out of the distance.

"Let me take that," the conductor said, taking my suitcase in one hand and using the other to help me down the two small stairs of the train. I stepped onto the platform and nodded my head. "Thanks."

"Pleasure," he said, winking at me and moving on to the next person.

"Maizon Singh?" A woman called, moving quickly toward me. Even though she was as big as Ms. Dell, she moved like a small person, taking smooth quick steps toward me, holding her hat with one hand and a purse with the other. She looked familiar and after a moment I realized she was in many of the pictures Grandma and I had pored over in the few months before.

"Ms. Bender?" I asked.

"Two hundred girls and you're my only load-up, Miss Maizon Singh," she said as I followed her over to the green station wagon she had parked beside the ticket window. "I guess you know I'm your dorm mom."

I nodded, shoving my suitcase into the backseat before climbing in beside her. The car smelled of peppermint and vinyl.

Ms. Bender looked over at me and smiled. "Hear tell, you know a whole lot, Maizon. Hook up."

I fastened my seat belt and stole another look at Ms. Bender as she pulled away from the ticket window. She drove slowly and carefully, the way Grandma used to drive before her legs starting getting sore. She had the most beautiful hair I had ever seen. It was long and black with streaks of gray and white running through it. Her skin was so pale, it looked like someone could just reach right through it; and her eyes were green, it seemed, then at another moment they looked gray or blue. I had never seen eyes change so.

"Dorm mothers live in your dorm," I said. "And kind of keep watch."

Ms. Bender nodded, checked her rearview mirror, then stared straight ahead again. We moved slowly past huge Victorian houses set back from bright green lawns. I pressed my palm against the half-closed window and let the warm air blow into my eyes.

"What kind of trees are those?" I pointed to a tree covered with pink, white, and lavender blossoms. "They're so beautiful."

"Mountain laurel, Maizon. And that sweet Connecticut air you're smelling is pine and beech and birch and elm. Come mid-October, the sky's going to catch on fire. All gold and red."

I inhaled. I had never smelled anything so wonderful. "Makes me think of fall just beginning to happen."

"Sure does. That last warm day coming at you when all you want to do is be outside in it."

After a moment, Ms. Bender patted my leg. "Don't look so doomed, Maizon. You'll make friends here."

I turned to her. "What are the girls like?"

She laughed softly, revealing small, even teeth with a gap like Grandma's between the two front ones. "A Blue Hill girl. That's like asking what Americans are like or what New Yorkers are like. There is every kind of girl here. Big ones, small ones, nice ones, and downright mean ones . . ."

"Are they all rich girls?"

Ms. Bender was silent for a moment. "I really couldn't tell you. Something seems to happen to a girl when she becomes a Chameleon—that's our mascot and insignia. I guess it's the same as what happens with the reptile—the girls change over into someone they weren't when they came here. I guess it's a little bad to say this, especially to a new arrival"—she looked over at me and smiled—"but I'm going to say it anyway. I think most of the girls are well off financially, being that the scholarship program is so new. But after a while, they seem to blend into something that's no longer about how much money they have or anything like that. No. It seems to me, it takes something more to become a Chameleon. And I'm not so sure what that something is."

I nodded, not understanding what Ms. Bender was getting at.

Chapter Six

When Ms. Bender pulled up in front of my dorm, Edwina Chapman Hall, I had to sit in the car a moment, not sure what my next move would be. The two-story redbrick building had long, straight rows of windows with black sills and flower boxes. Some of the boxes had zinnias and geraniums growing out of them. Others were empty. Trees lined the side of the building and a redbrick path led right up to a huge black door. I looked up. There were groups of girls pressed against various windows. When I looked in their direction, some waved, some ducked behind their curtains.

"I have the rest of the afternoon off, Maizon," Ms. Bender said after a few moments had passed. "Mrs. Miller takes it from here. Go on upstairs and meet whoever's up there. Don't forget, there's an orientation in the main hall this evening."

I climbed out and lifted my bag from the backseat. "Thanks for picking me up and everything, Ms. Bender."

Ms. Bender waved her hand. "My pleasure. Such a nice day for a drive. Glad to have you to share it with."

I nodded, closed the door, and moved away from the car.

"You just settle in, Maizon," Ms. Bender called, pulling slowly away from the dorm. "And get yourself ready for a year of learning." She waved and drove off down the small dirt road that led back up to a big white building that I knew from pictures was the main hall.

Not looking up at the windows again, I walked straight up to the door and pushed my shoulder against it. It gave easily and a rush of cool air moved through the dim hallway. Marble stairs led up to the second floor. I moved slowly past the quiet doors looking for the one with 204 in brass letters across it. My new loafers squeaked with each step in the hushed hallways and the sound of the quiet echoed back over itself. It is strange how loud quiet can be sometimes. There was so much space, it seemed, even though the hall wasn't that wide. It was as if the quiet made the space bigger somehow.

"Are you Mizon Sigg?"

I turned around. Behind me stood a girl with dark shades, twirling a thick braid around her finger. It didn't surprise me that she was black, because of the way she said my name and the hoarseness of her voice. What I hadn't expected to see was someone with dark-tinted glasses who was a lot taller than me.

"Maizon Singh," I said. "First name rhymes with raisin. Second name rhymes with ring."

"Maizon Singh," she repeated, coming closer. "I'm Dana Charlesetta King. Everybody calls me Charli though. Well, everybody *here* calls me Charli. At home, I'm Dana."

"Hi, Charli."

"I was just in Sheila and Marie's room. We saw you out the window. I told them I'd come get you so that we could all be introduced. I figured we could all walk over to the main hall together. I'm pretty orientated out. They make us do this every year. But dinner follows. We all can sit together."

"Who's 'we all'?" I cocked an eyebrow at her.

Charli pulled her shades up and rolled her eyes, then looked over her shoulder quickly. "The colored folks, girlfriend. All four of us, now. Well . . . actually there's five, but . . . anyway." Charli grabbed my hand. "Leave your suitcase here. It's safe. You won't be needing anything in it anyway. Once you get your uniform, all you'll be needing is a clean body to put it on. Come on."

"I wanted to see my room and say hi to my roommate," I said, pulling back.

"Your roommate won't be back until later on tonight. And if you see one room you've seen them all. So see Sheila and Marie's. They're probably cleaning off a spot for you anyway. Talk about slobs."

Charli was wearing a T-shirt and a pair of the shortest shorts I had ever seen.

"Those are nice boots," I said, pointing to the black shin-high lace-ups she was wearing with white socks.

"I practically had to cut off a foot to get them. My mother and dad said they look too rough. Like combat boots. But I explained that I'd only be able to wear them on weekends and holidays anyway, so they let me get them. I'm a junior this year, so I think they're starting to lay off me a bit."

I pushed my suitcase against the wall and followed Charli, hoping Marie and Sheila weren't as talkative as she was.

"It's sure quiet here."

Charli laughed loudly, throwing her head back, so her braid bounced against her neck. She looked at me, raising her shades again. Her eyes were dark. She had the longest lashes of anybody I had ever seen. "That's why I'm here, girlfriend. This year I'm going to make some noise! Blue Hill is *not* ready for Dana-Charlesetta-call-me-Charli King."

I giggled. We passed room 210. Bruce Springsteen was singing "Born in the U.S.A." behind the door.

"What about Ms. Bender?"

Charli looked over her shoulder again. "Bender Spender," she said softly. "You know, she was married to a black guy for years and years. She has two half-black sons. Those boys are *fine*!" Charli said, kissing her fingers.

"What happened to her husband?"

She grabbed my shoulder and stopped, raising her shades to look me straight in the eye. "That's the dirt," she said slowly. "Her husband was some sort of revolutionary-type guy. He woke up one day and looked over and saw Ms. Bender lying there beside him and realized he was married to a white woman. I guess the revolution he was fighting wasn't ready for interracial marriage. He got out of bed and ran down to city hall—changed his name to some back-to-Africa something and filed for a divorce. I guess the divorce room was right next door to the name-change place."

"That's so stupid," I said. "Like he didn't know it before?"

In the one picture I have of my mother and father together, my mother looks pale against my father's dark brown skin. I wondered then if he'd ever awakened and saw my mother different than when he first fell in love with her. I wondered if he maybe thought she was too light for him. I shook my head. He stayed with my mother until she died having me. Then he left. His leaving had something to do with me, not my mother. "That's so stupid," I said again.

"Yeah," Charli agreed. "But it makes good dirt. And wait till you meet those boys!"

"Ms. Bender seems real nice," I said. We had stopped and were standing outside room 242. It was at the end of the hall. We were still whispering.

"She's sweet. I kind of feel bad that I'm going to give her so much grief this year," Charli said. She pressed the shades up on her nose and grinned.

Chapter Seven

"Marie, Sheila . . . Maizon Singh." Charli held out her hand and bowed in my direction.

"Hi," Marie and Sheila said in unison. They were sitting side by side on a narrow bed, looking through a photo album that seemed to be filled with pictures of one boy. I pushed a pile of clothes out of the way and sat on the bed across from them. Half-empty suitcases cluttered the floor, but framed pictures of the boy in the photo album were hung neatly on the wall behind the bed.

"I'm Marie," the taller girl said, looking me up and down in a way that made me feel like I was dressed wrong. I ran my fingers through my hair and said nothing.

"And this is Cleo, Marie's boyfriend." Charli smirked, gesturing toward the photographs on the wall. "And that's Cleo," she said again, pointing toward the photo album that Marie and Sheila were drooling over. "Expect to see a lot of him—well, a lot of pictures. A *college* man."

"He is so utterly fine, Marie," Sheila said, tearing her eyes away from the photo album to glance at me. "Hi, Maizon." She turned the page of the photo album. More bright pictures of Cleo jumped off the black pages. He was cute, I guess, with a big smile and stuffed cheeks like a squirrel.

"Wow! What a body!" Sheila giggled, pointing at a picture of Cleo in his bathing trunks. He was a little on the thin side, to me, with tiny muscles moving down his arms and long, skinny legs.

"We've been going out three months now," Marie said. "I think I'm in love!"

The three of them squealed and giggled, reminding me of Li'l Jay. I rolled my eyes. Boys bored the heck out of me.

"Well," Charli announced, "Peter and I've been seeing each other eight months."

"Peter's S-T-A-L-E, Charli. He is so boring." Sheila's eyes lit up when she said this. She looked over at me and winked.

"At least I have a boyfriend to call my own."

"You don't have a boyfriend," Sheila teased. "You have a pet."

They all laughed and cooed over a few more pictures of Cleo.

Then Marie shut the book and turned to me. "I'm a junior," she announced. "So's Charli, but I guess she's already told you that."

"I'm a sophomore," Sheila said. "Three more years in this place."

"And you just got here, Maizon," Charli said, bouncing down next to me. She had more energy than Li'l Jay. "Buckle your seat belt, girlfriend, 'cause you in for one heck of a ride."

"Charli. You're slipping," Marie said, frowning.

"Oh, chill out, Marie." Charli waved her hand and lay back on the bed. "We're among our own."

The room was smaller than I had expected, with dark wood twin bureaus at the head of the beds. Heavy gray curtains hung at the windows. The floor had been tiled in gray and white with the white tiles matching the walls. I looked at the pink-and-gray throw rugs at the foot of each bed.

"We brought those from home," Marie said. "To give this place some color."

"So you're from Brooklyn?" Sheila asked, folding her hands in her lap. I didn't like the way she said it, like Brooklyn was a place at the end of the map that no one in her right mind would ever go to.

I nodded.

"I've never been there," she continued. "My family's traveled to New York though. And my dad has a cousin or uncle or something that used to or still lives in Brooklyn."

"It's bad there, isn't it?" Marie asked. "Lots of killings and stuff?"

"*New York* is bad," Sheila piped in. "Don't you

read the papers? They're only written on a third-grade level."

"Actually," I said, '*The New York Times* is written at a seventh-grade level. Most of the tabloids are written below that. The *Times* is more informative. No comics though."

The room fell silent. I had raised my foot up to the edge of the bed and was playing with the penny in one of my loafers, turning it from heads to tails then back again. When I looked up, all three of them were staring at me.

Marie studied her hands. Her fingers were long, the color of dark toast, and she had polished her nails pale pink.

"I'm from California," she said. "Santa Cruz. Halfway around the world. Have you ever been there?" Her voice was soft and even. It scared me.

I shook my head.

"Ever been to California?" she asked. Sheila and Charli were silent. I looked at Charli. I couldn't tell if her eyes were open or not behind the shades. Sheila's hair was in a million tiny braids that hung down to her shoulder. She pulled one over her eyes and started unbraiding it.

I shook my head. "Never been outside of New York. This is my first time."

"None of us is on scholarship, Maizon," Marie continued.

I shrugged. "So? What's that supposed to mean?"

"Ooohee!" Charli squealed. "This girl's got *attitude*! I like that."

"I don't have attitude," I said casually. "I just don't want anybody in my face telling me what they are and aren't."

"I just thought I'd inform you," Marie said. "Just so you don't think *all* the blacks here are broke."

I rolled my eyes at Marie. "My family's not broke. This is an academic scholarship."

"Whatever," Marie said, sounding bored. She brushed something from her lap, and for a moment, I got the eerie feeling that she was brushing *me* off.

"Humph," Sheila grunted, still working the braid. "Wish I was on scholarship. This school is *stupid* expensive."

"Sheila!"

"Oh, give it a break, Marie. It's just us."

"It's just us now, but what happens when we let it go, forgetting who is around us?"

"Let what go?" I asked. Out past Marie's and Sheila's heads I could see the blue hill. The sun was sinking bright orange behind it. A group of girls were fooling around at the top.

"Marie's going to major in language. She has to stay on her toes," Charli said.

Marie nodded. "I'm interested in the different

ways people have of speaking around each other. I'm either going to Harvard, Yale, or Brown."

"Oh," I said. "Those are good schools." I still didn't like Marie, but I wanted to show her that I knew about colleges.

"So are Morehouse, Spelman, and Howard," Charli said.

"They're not Ivy League though," Marie said.

"They're *black* league, girl." Charli raised herself up on her elbows. "Black schools for black people. Get your education and culture"—Charli snapped her finger—"under one roof."

Marie sucked her teeth and walked over to the window. She looked as though she could be six feet tall. Her Levi's were tapered super straight the way I had tried to get Grandma to make mine. But she had insisted my feet wouldn't be able to get through the bottom if she made them any straighter than they were. Marie was wearing a white turtleneck T-shirt. I pulled my shirt away from my chest, feeling little and flat-chested.

"This is the same tired old argument—"

"Tired old argument? You're slipping, Marie." Sheila and Charli slapped palms, laughing.

"Marie thinks we shouldn't use the 'tired old language' of black folks and should speak—What's the word, Marie? 'Correctly'?"

"I think the way we speak says a lot about who we are," Marie said, turning her back to the window and folding her arms. "People judge you by it."

"But that is who we *are*?" Charli said, raising her shades. "You better take some courses in the *history* of language, girl, before you start working to change it."

Sheila nodded.

I wasn't sure I understood what they were talking about. Ms. Dell spoke differently from Margaret and me. So did Hattie. And Grandma and Ms. Dell spoke differently when they were together than when Grandma was speaking to Mr. Parsons.

"What do you think, Maizon?" Charli asked. Someone giggled in the hallway. I pulled my knees up to my chin and stared out past Marie. I liked the sun in Connecticut. It seemed cleaner than Brooklyn sun.

"Language is fluid," I said softly. "It changes—I mean the way we speak. The way black people speak changes. I don't think one way is right or the other way is wrong as long as you can get your point across."

Marie sucked her teeth and turned back to the window. Sheila looked at me and shrugged.

"You have a lot to learn, Maizon," Marie said.

"Then I'll learn it," I said, feeling a little less afraid of her. "I'll learn *everything*."

Charli giggled and lay back down on the bed. "You two sure are slobs. Look at this room."

"We're unpacking, Chuck," Sheila said. She rose and began putting underwear and socks into her bureau.

Marie continued to stare out the window, silent.

"I'm from Detroit, Maizon," Charli said. "Doctor's daughter."

"You're from Southfield, Charli. Southfield, Michigan, is a bit of a cry from Detroit."

"It's a car ride away."

"Exactly," Sheila laughed. "A car ride. Which means you don't have to get on a *bus,* like the people in Detroit, to get there."

"Her family," Charli said to me, pointing to Sheila, "is one of two black families in Cherryville. You know where that is, don't you?"

I nodded. Cherryville is a rich suburb of New York.

"And because of it," Sheila said, "I'm headed straight for Spelman—the bestest blackest college on the map! You can have your Harvards and your Yales."

"I can't believe you're going to waste a straight *A* average on Spelman," Marie said.

"I can't believe you're going to waste your melanin on Ivy League!" Sheila retorted, folding a bra and placing it in the top drawer.

I listened to them bicker, liking the way their voices moved through all the quiet. I felt hungry for something. It wasn't food. I didn't know what it was, but knew it had something to do with their arguing and laughter and snapping fingers and something to do with the way the sun was setting outside the window. And even a little bit to do with Bruce Springsteen down the hall shouting that he was born in the U.S.A.

Chapter Eight

When I got to my room, I went straight to the window and pulled my curtains open. The blue hill was almost gray against the dusk. I raised my window and pressed my hand against the screen. It was warm outside. A breeze rushed past and I pressed my face against the screen, trying to catch the last of it. Four girls walked past the dorm, holding hands. I swallowed, wondering if Margaret had already found a new best friend she could walk around with. Home. They would all be sitting on the stoop now—Ms. Dell and Hattie and Margaret and Li'l Jay—catching the last bit of daytime. I leaned against the windowsill, scraping my nails slowly up and down the screen. Mr. Parsons hadn't lied after all. There were other black girls here. But they were older than me, and somehow different. Marie and Charli and Sheila. And Charli had mentioned another one too. But there was something about her Charli wasn't saying. I wondered who she was and what it was that had turned Charli against her.

"It's what I've always wanted for you, Maizon," Grandma said when she got the news that I had gotten into Blue Hill. The information came in a thick white envelope. Since then, I'd come to think that thick white envelopes meant good news and thin ones meant bad, depending on how you look at it.

"A good school. One of the best schools," Mr. Parsons had said, giving me a thin, scared-looking smile. I'd figured somebody touched up his photographs to make Blue Hill look like more than it was. But this place was the place in the pictures—all green and gold and blue. Blue Hill was beautiful, the way the school grounds were scattered with mountain laurel. Even the way the sun dipped down behind the hill and all the grass everywhere. The small cobblestone paths that led up to the different buildings made the school look ancient and rich, like a thousand millionaires had built it from an old memory of something. Still, I couldn't figure out what the empty place at the center of my stomach was about. It made my legs weak, even made me aware of how my toes felt inside my loafers.

There was a knock at the door. I came away from the window and busied myself with my suitcase. "Come in."

"Maizon?" A woman peeked around the corner

of the door, then stepped in. Another woman followed her and closed the door.

"You might remember me from the interview. . . ." the first woman said.

"Mrs. Miller." I walked over and shook her hand firmly, the way Grandma had said I should do with adults.

Mrs. Miller nodded. "I live in this dorm with my husband. We're right downstairs if you need anything. I'm sure you know Ms. Bender is on the third floor. One or the other of us is always around. This is Miss Norman," Mrs. Miller said. Miss Norman took a step toward me. She was kind of heavy and only a little taller than me with short black-and-gray hair. I stared at her a moment, because she couldn't have been much older than Hattie. The gray hair looked strange against her young face. She was pretty. When I reached to shake her hand, Miss Norman winked at me. I wondered if she was winking because we were almost the same height or because we were both black.

"Nice to meet you, Maizon," Miss Norman said. Her voice was so soft, it surprised me. And without thinking, I immediately loosened my grip on her hand.

She laughed and I felt the heat rise up to my face.

"I used to sing," Miss Norman said. "I'm used to people being surprised at such a small voice coming out of such a big body. Don't worry. It's not a sign of weakness."

I nodded, not knowing what to say.

"Mind if we sit down?" Mrs. Miller asked, sitting down on the bed across from mine and running her palm across the wrinkles in the dark blue blanket. The beds were identical, right down to the white sheets and blue-flowered pillowcases. I had chosen the one closer to the window.

Miss Norman pulled a chair away from one of the two small desks against the wall and brought it up to the foot of the bed. She was wearing jeans, sneakers, and a T-shirt that had Blue Hill Chameleons in bright orange-and-black letters across the front.

I closed my suitcase and sat down on a small corner of the bed.

"So, how're you settling in, Maizon?" Mrs. Miller asked, crossing her legs and pulling her dress down around her knees.

I shrugged. "Fine, I guess. This school is pretty."

"Scary, isn't it?" Miss Norman leaned forward a little, resting her elbows on her knees. A glint came into her eyes when she smiled.

I nodded. "I met some people already. Charli and Sheila . . . and Marie."

Mrs. Miller gave a small laugh. "Blue Hill's own welcoming committee. . . . Did Charli try to recruit you for our field-hockey team yet?"

"I don't know how to play."

"That's not a problem. Miss Norman is the best coach this school has seen in I don't know how long—field hockey *and* basketball."

"You play *basketball*?" I couldn't believe it. In Brooklyn, even the girls' basketball coaches had been men.

Miss Norman held up one of her feet. "This year's sneaker," she said about the red-on-white Nike high-top. "The whole team will have them. B-ball doesn't start until winter though. Nice shoes, huh?"

I nodded. I'd always loved high-tops.

"Think about joining, Maizon. Junior varsity could use some new blood."

I shrugged. The last thing I wanted was to look spastic in front of a bunch of strangers. "Maybe . . ."

"Well," Mrs. Miller said, "there's also the debate team and track, and of course, the Blue Hill *Journal*. That's our school paper. I hear you like to write."

"Yes. But I think I'm going to need to study a lot—"

"There'll be plenty of time to study," Mrs. Miller said quickly. "Ask any student here. And I'll be happy to tutor you in math if you need it."

I shook my head. "I'm taking advanced math—Algebra Two. Tested into it."

She nodded. "Then I'll be seeing plenty of you. I'm teaching that class this year."

Miss Norman slapped her thighs and rose. "Think about field hockey, Maizon. I'd love to have you on the team. And feel free to come over and talk to me. I'm in the English Department when I'm not on the field."

"What do you teach?"

Miss Norman grimaced. "British literature this year. Any interest in *Beowulf*?"

I giggled. "I like Grendel better than Beowulf. And the Green Knight better than Sir Gawain."

"My goodness!" Mrs. Miller said, raising her eyebrows. "When did you do all of this reading?"

I swallowed, looking down at my loafers. "I spent a lot of time reading when I was at home. Sometimes that was all I had to do. I don't really like television. So I had a contest with myself. I went to the library and tried to read all the fiction that I could pronounce the titles of. But last summer I didn't get to read so much. I was spending a lot of time with my friend, Margaret. Then her father died and she started spending more and more time with her family. I went back to reading when Margaret wasn't around. That's why I'm here, I guess. Everybody thinks I should keep learning more and more."

For a moment neither teacher said a word.

Then Miss Norman's soft voice floated through the silence. "We're here for you to talk to, Maizon.

The first few weeks are the hardest. I think you can get through them though. Especially if you think about playing field hockey!"

I looked up to see Mrs. Miller grinning.

Miss Norman winked at me again. "We're sort of what Charli, Sheila, and Marie are aspiring to be—the welcoming committee."

"Did the girls tell you that your roommate will be here later this evening?" she asked.

I nodded.

"Her name is Sandra—Sandy. She's in her second year here. I think you two will get along well."

"Is Charli still wearing those shades?" Miss Norman asked.

I laughed and nodded.

"I tell you," she said. "That girl is going to take them off one day and not have any eyes behind them!"

Chapter Nine

"Come on, Maizon," Charli called, reaching for my hand and nearly dragging me to catch up with Marie and Sheila. I had changed into my uniform because we weren't allowed to go into the dining hall in regular clothes. The green skirt felt strange flapping against my bare thighs and the Peter Pan collar on the white shirt we had to wear was tight around my neck. My favorite part of the whole uniform was the patch on the pocket of the green-and-black plaid blazer, with the gold thread that spelled out "Blue Hill." Charli, Sheila, and Marie's uniforms were different. Because they were in the upper school, they got to wear boxy blue plaid blazers and dark blue skirts. I wanted a blazer like theirs, but Charli had explained that the school gave them bigger blazers to hide their breasts. Blue Hill didn't think it had to worry about that problem with lower school freshmen. They were right. My blazer fell in a flat line across my chest. Even the white shirt underneath it didn't cause it to bulk.

We were walking across the field that separated our dorm from the main hall and I had dropped behind the others to watch the way the sun set behind the hill. It was so pretty, I thought I'd start crying. I wanted to tell someone about it, but I didn't know Charli and them well enough. Clusters of girls were emerging from the other dorms, making their way to the dining hall. "Dinner doesn't wait for anyone around here," Charli said, pressing her shades up on her nose.

The four of us entered the dining hall together, and for a moment, I felt like we were banding together against everyone. I wasn't sure if I was going to make any friends here, but I didn't want to risk it by hanging with just Marie, Sheila, and Charli.

The dining hall was big and warm. There were about twenty tables all set with white tablecloths, off-white plates, and silver. Black-and-white rag rugs were laid out in the aisles between the tables. Logs sat at the far corner beside a huge fireplace.

"Sit at our table," Marie said. "It's over there." She pointed to the corner table and then went off to speak to a group of older girls huddled in the corner.

"You have to serve tonight, Charli," Mrs. Miller said as we sat down. "With or without the shades."

Charli scowled, then headed off to the kitchen, leaving Sheila and me alone at the table.

"I think you're going to like Blue Hill, Maizon. It's a good school. It's hard on some kids. But it all depends on what you came here for." Sheila shrugged. "Me, I just came here to get some good learning before I head off for Spelman." She picked up a fork and twirled it on the table. "Sometimes, I hate this place."

"You just said it's not so bad."

Sheila looked at me like she was about to say something, then caught herself and started twirling her fork again. "You'll see what it's like, Maizon," she said slowly. "Then you'll know what I mean."

I pulled out a chair at the head of the table and sat down. Then turned in my seat to see the other girls. Everyone seemed to know each other.

"Somebody sock you, Charli?" someone called across the dining hall. Charli set a basket of bread on our table, then raised her shades and winked in the direction of the voice.

"It's this year's look," Charli said, heading back toward the kitchen. Another girl came out and set a plate of chicken on the table across from ours.

The dining hall was filling up quickly. I had never seen so many girls together in one place.

"Hi, Maizon." A brown-haired girl stood at the edge of our table. "I'm Sandy, your roommate."

"Hi," I said. My heart sank a bit. I'd been hoping Sandy would be black.

"Hi, Sheila. Happy autumn."

Without lifting her head, Sheila waved in the direction of Sandy's voice.

"Well . . . I guess I'll see you back at the room later, Maizon."

I nodded. "Later, Sandy."

We were the only ones sitting at our table, which was set for six.

"Black bonding," Marie said to me, pulling a chair out at the other end of the table. "It's good for the spirit."

I served myself a piece of chicken, some peas, and a spoonful of rice. I chewed slowly, liking the newness of the food. The chicken could've used some salt and the rice was a little dry, but I was starving, so it didn't matter.

"Pass me the bread, please," Sheila said.

I took a dinner roll and passed the basket to Sheila.

Marie looked annoyed. "Maizon, you don't serve yourself when you're passing the food. You let the other person help themselves first. Otherwise, it's rude."

"Oh, kill it, Marie. I don't mind." Sheila took a roll, broke off a piece, and buttered it.

"I do things *my* way, Marie." I laid my fork beside my plate and glared at her. She glared back. "If I want a piece of bread, I take it."

"It's rude. It means you have no home training."

"I don't care if it means I paint my nails green. It's my way of doing it, and to me, that's how it's done!"

Marie glared at me a moment longer, then stuffed a forkful of peas in her mouth.

I tore my roll in half, buttered it, and crammed the whole half into my mouth.

"There's Pauli," Sheila said, motioning her head in the direction of the door.

A black girl was walking briskly toward a table at the far end of the dining hall.

"Oreo," Marie muttered under her breath.

"What grade is she in?" I asked hopefully. Pauli looked about my age. Maybe a little older.

"It doesn't matter," Charli said, rolling her eyes. "Pauli doesn't hang with sisters."

"She's *assimilated,*" Marie added, snidely.

Pauli had thrown her head back and was laughing with the group of white girls sitting at her table. They stared at her adoringly.

I picked up another piece of chicken with my fingers and dared Marie to say something.

Charli turned to me. "Pauli really doesn't hang with us, so it doesn't matter what grade she's in."

"Sort of sad," Sheila added. "She's way disconnected. Every time Blue Hill does something like a black history month celebration or bringing a black woman up to speak for women's history month, Pauli never gets involved. It's like she doesn't want to face the fact that she's black."

"Maybe she's just not interested in those things," I suggested.

Charli raised her shades and crossed her eyes at me. "Maybe she just doesn't deal."

I shrugged. What they were saying made me even more interested in Pauli.

"Speaking of dealing," Sheila cut in, "Cadman is having a dance this winter."

They all squealed and giggled. Charli blew a kiss at nothing, then laughed.

"Cadman's the boys' school in the next town, Maizon," Sheila explained. "Do they have some fine numbers going there!"

"Remember Ron? Brown skinned, brown eyed baby-cakes?" Charli closed her eyes. "Man, could that boy turn a slow dance into a dangerous thing!"

"And Curtis, who graduated last year? I'm gonna write him," Marie added.

"Marie, you already have a college boy. No stockpiling." Sheila laughed, elbowing Marie.

I hated the way girls got silly-eyed over boys. I didn't get it. Something about boys made even the smartest girls seem dumber than tree stumps.

"We'll hook you up with someone nice, Maizon," Charli offered.

"No interest, Charli."

They all looked at me, saying nothing. Then

Charli smiled. "Don't worry. I didn't have an interest either. Then one day I woke up and boom! —the boys were all right!

"Anyway," Charli added, rising, "We're having chocolate cake for dessert."

"What does that have to do with guys?" Marie asked.

"I don't know." Charli lifted her glass of milk to her mouth and drained it. "Figured since we're so smart, maybe we could make some sort of connection."

I giggled and forked the last bit of rice into my mouth before handing my empty plate to Charli.

After dinner, I walked slowly back from the dining hall by myself, wanting to take in Connecticut without anybody else around. A group of girls giggled past me, their Blue Hill jackets draped across their shoulders. One girl turned and waved and I waved back without smiling.

The sky was the color of ink. Black like my mother's eyes in the pictures Grandma had on the mantelpiece back home. Stars speckled it with tiny dots of light. I stopped in the middle of the field and clenched my eyes against the tears I knew would come if I let them. The air blowing against my face was cool. I swallowed big gulps of it. There was something I wanted to consume. I was thinking about my father; only, he wasn't like the man in the picture with Mama. That man was tall with skin the color of autumn—all golden-brown and soft—and curly hair. The man that came to mind was Margaret's father—Mr. Tory—even though he died last summer. Mr. Tory was blocking out the image of my father. I walked slowly, swallowing every few steps, my head thrown back against the breeze. An awful loneliness came over me, working its way up from the middle of my stomach to the center of my chest. I needed to picture my father and I couldn't. I hated him so much for leaving me. Hated him like I've never ever hated anybody. Margaret was lucky. She had a word for what her father was. Death was something solid—something with a name and place to it. Something certain. But for where my father was, I didn't have anything. I didn't know if he would ever show up again. The only thing I was sure of was that he had come to Grandma's house on a cold day in April with me bundled up in blankets. He had me in one arm and a suitcase in the other.

"I can't take care of her," he had whispered to Grandma, handing me over.

And then he was gone, taking with him one big suitcase and the face my mother had fallen in love with. The thought of him drifts back and forth and I'm always wondering if he'll return. Sometimes I pray that he doesn't. And sometimes I hope he will. I wish on falling stars and eyelashes. Absence isn't solid the way death is. It's fluid, like language. And it hurts so much . . . so, so much.

* * *

A mosquito buzzed closed to the side of my head and I shooed it away. "Eeny, meeny miney mo . . ." I sang softly to myself. Somewhere far off, bells were ringing. I walked through the grass, feeling the earth go soft beneath my loafers. "Let's catch Maizon by her toes. If she hollers, don't let her go. . . . Eeny Meeny Miney Mo. . . ."

Something was missing. I wondered if Blue Hill was the beginning of something always being missing.

Chapter Ten

"Maizon, can I borrow your soap?" I wrapped my towel tighter around me. Claudette stood in front of me, stark naked. I'd met her at orientation last night.

The bathroom was big, with three showers and four toilet stalls. But I had never had to share a bathroom with anyone, and standing on the cold tile with other girls brushing their teeth at the sink and one in front of me stark naked was something I'd never imagined myself doing.

I handed Claudette the plastic soap container.

"Thanks," she said, darting toward the shower. "I left mine back in my room." I walked over to a sink that was freed up by a girl I didn't know who had been blow-drying her hair in front of it, and started combing my hair. Around me, other girls went about their morning duties in various stages of undress. Most of them just had on bras and panties. Even if I wore a bra, I wouldn't walk around in it with nothing else on. I looked at my skinny shoulders in the mirror. I didn't even have one pubic hair. Sharing or no sharing, I wasn't about to let the girls see how undeveloped I was.

"You can give it to me later," I called to Claudette, gathering my stuff together.

"Thanks," she yelled back over the running water.

Back in my room, I dressed slowly, then tried to get some more unpacking done. Sandy had already left, so I had the room all to myself for a few minutes. My tour person would be coming at nine. But at eight forty-five, there was a knock on the door.

"I'm Susan," a brown-haired girl with glasses said. "I've been assigned to show you around. I'm a junior here."

"I'm Maizon," I said, moving aside to let her in. "Make yourself comfortable. I was doing a little unpacking."

"I'm kind of in a rush," Susan said, brushing past me and sitting on Sandy's bed.

I hung a pair of sweatpants in the closet, then folded a T-shirt and put it in the dresser drawer at the head of my bed. "I guess this can wait until we come back. . . ."

Susan watched my hands as I worked and I wondered what she could be thinking. I had seen her in the cafeteria last night, but hadn't paid much attention to her. She was shorter than I was, with a face that sort of pinched itself into a frown.

"You remind me of the lady who works for my family," Susan said. "She has her hair like yours —cut short. And she folds and hangs everything up carefully like you. Her last name is Peterson. You know her?"

I shook my head.

"I thought maybe you guys were related." Susan leaned back on her elbows and eyed the room. "My room's bigger than this."

"Yeah, so's Marie and Sheila's down the hall. They say lower school freshmen get the short end of the stick around here."

"I thought they gave you a cheapie room 'cause you're on scholarship, since you're not really contributing to the cost."

I shrugged. "It doesn't bother me. I don't need a lot of space." I started counting to ten in my head, because Grandma had said I should do that before deciding I didn't like a person. She said sometimes by the time you get to seven, you're already liking the person more.

"What does your father do?" Susan asked, too casually.

"He's a lawyer." I was up to eight now, and because she had made me lie, I was sure I didn't like her. I wasn't about to tell Susan the real story of my father.

"Corporate or public interest?" Susan asked.

"Public interest," I said quickly, trying not to stutter.

"Criminal?"

"Huh?"

"Is he a criminal lawyer?"

"Uh-huh," I nodded.

"That's too bad. My dad's a prosecutor. He tries to get as many criminals off the street as he can. He thinks criminal lawyers should be behind bars too."

"Not everybody's guilty."

"Yeah, yeah . . . that's what they all say."

"Sometimes cops make mistakes."

"Rarely."

I clinched my fist over a pair of lavender socks. What right did this girl have coming into my room and making me lie about my life, anyway?

"I don't want to talk about it," I said, lowering my voice.

"It's a losing argument." Susan stood up and came over to the dresser. "Who's this?" she asked, pointing to the picture Hattie took last summer. In it, me and Margaret were standing with our arms across each other's shoulders.

"That's my best friend, Margaret."

"She's pretty. I think some black people are real pretty, you know. Like, they have real clear skin and nice teeth. Where are her parents boarding her?"

"Huh?"

"What school is she at?"

"P.S. 102 . . . in Brooklyn."

"Public school?"

I nodded. I had learned to fight when I was seven and Michael Acosta tried to bully me and Margaret into giving him our snack money. After I beat him up, I wasn't scared of anyone anymore. Michael had been a whole head taller than me. It wouldn't take much at all to pound Susan into the ground. I started counting again. Everyone deserved a second chance.

"That's frightening. Don't they kill people every day in those schools?"

"You must be reading the *National Enquirer* or something," I said, letting a little of my annoyance seep into my voice.

"No, my father told me that. He said New York schools are dangerous."

"Give me a break. Next time you talk to your father, ask him when was the last time he was in one."

"Don't get snotty," Susan said. "I was just repeating what I heard."

I shrugged. "Well, think before you say it. People will think you're a parrot. Anyway, I'm ready for my tour," I said, holding the door open.

Susan looked in the mirror and finger-combed some hair out of her eyes before heading for the door.

Susan was a pain, but she gave a thorough tour.

By the time we were finished, I felt like I knew Blue Hill inside and out.

"I've been giving freshman tours since my second year here," Susan said, when she dropped me off at my dorm. "You could probably pass a test on the history of Blue Hill now."

I thanked her bluntly—wanting her to understand that while I appreciated the tour, I still didn't like her. She got the point, I think, because she looked confused for a moment, then turned on her heel and headed back across the field.

"Hi, Maizon."

Ms. Bender was sitting in the first-floor lounge. In the corner, a huge fireplace sat unlit with logs beside it. The chair she sat in was one of those comfortable overstuffed ones with flowered upholstery. Lace doilies were thrown across the arms and back. "Figured I could catch up on some reading. How was the tour?"

I took a seat in the chair across from her. "It was okay. This is a pretty place."

Ms. Bender nodded. "People say that. I'm glad you think so too." She lay the magazine across her lap and leaned forward. "How's Susan?"

I grimaced.

Ms. Bender chuckled. "I know what you mean," she said, but didn't volunteer any other information. "I told you, we have all kinds of girls here. But isn't diversity important?"

"I guess."

"We learn from each other that way."

I was silent for a moment. I guess Susan and I did learn some things from each other today. I learned that she wasn't the brightest girl that ever walked the earth and she learned that she had better not mess with me.

A tall boy blasted through the door and ran up to Ms. Bender's chair, then stumbled to a stop. He was the color of caramel, with light brown eyes and short curly hair. My heart skipped as I realized I hadn't seen a boy in days. I hadn't even missed them!

"Mama," he said, out of breath, "I don't think I'm staying the weekend after all."

Ms. Bender nodded knowingly. "This is my younger son, Davis," she said to me. "Davis, this is Maizon."

Davis looked over at me and smiled. A thin line of silver ran across his already straight teeth. "Hi, Maizon!"

I swallowed, trying to figure out where my tongue had run off to. "Hi . . . Davis," I stuttered. Charli had been right. He was *fine.*

"Davis is a college man now." Ms. Bender sighed. "No more time for Mama."

Davis looked embarrassed for a moment. "Ma, they're putting some guys on line tonight. I have to get back."

"A fraternity man," Ms. Bender continued, then turned to Davis. "Well, get on back and pledge those poor boys. But don't forget you were once *on line.*"

Davis left as quickly as he had come. Ms. Bender fanned herself with the magazine. " 'On line' is what they do in those fraternities and sororities. Once you're on line, you're on your way to whatever it means to be a frat brother or sorority sister. Doesn't make a whole lot of sense to me. But . . . whatever."

I smiled, still starry-eyed.

Ms. Bender took one look at me and laughed. "Join the crowd of Blue Hill girls in love with him, Maizon," she said. "He knows he has a fan club here. But forget it! He's twenty years old. And his brother, who is just as beautiful, is twenty-seven."

I shrugged. "I don't think about boys that much," I confided. "I hadn't even missed them until Davis walked in."

"Well, you're a lone soldier here then. But you have time. I give you about a year and a half. Then they'll fill every inch of your conversation."

I doubted it. But I didn't tell Ms. Bender that. I liked reading and double-dutch and good gossip. I liked learning new stuff about life and twirling the info around in my head for days and days. Davis was cute. But he wouldn't stay on my mind long. I wanted to know about Ms. Bender and the husband that left her. I was way into learning about people leaving.

"Where's your other son?"

"Moved to Seattle. He's an activist. You name the problem, he'll fight to change it." She smiled to herself. "Just like his father . . ." she mumbled, shaking her head.

"Are you divorced?" I asked, even though I already knew the answer.

Ms. Bender nodded, but didn't say anything. I wondered how Charli had gotten the information out of her.

After a few minutes had passed in silence, I smiled and got up. "I guess I'll call my grandma and write some letters."

"Big day tomorrow," Ms. Bender warned. "Ready, set, go."

I walked around her and bounded up the stairs, liking the way the cool wood banister felt against my palm.

"Easy on those stairs, Maizon," Ms. Bender called. "Don't stomp. You'll go right through to the basement."

I giggled, because my grandma always said the same thing.

Chapter Eleven

Dear Margaret,

I met a girl named Susan the other day. She's a junior here. She's never really known any black people. She thinks we're too different from whites and maybe shouldn't mingle so much. I guess some of the girls here feel that way. Sometimes it makes me angry thinking about it, but most of the time I just feel real, real sorry for them.

You've written me two letters already. I know you want to know what it's like here, but there are some things you can't even explain to a best friend. I know you wouldn't understand this Blue Hill thing. I'm not saying you're not smart or anything. But it's just like how it is about Mama. Nobody, not even Grandma, understands that I knew her. Remember how Grandma would laugh when I said I knew Mama? Remember how she would say, "You couldn't have known her, Maizon. You were a baby then. You had not been in this world an hour when your mama died."

But somewhere, way down deep inside of me, Margaret, I remember that hour. I remember bright lights and voices and dark faces over me. I remember lots of white and green. And nobody knows this, nobody would ever in a million years believe this, but I do remember my mama. I remember her looking just the way she looks in all the pictures Grandma has of her over the fireplace and in the bedroom. Mama had long, long hair and those high cheekbones like Grandma's. And even when *you* look at the pictures, Margaret, you say I have my mama's mouth—just like in the pictures. And I have Mama's nose too. I used to didn't like my nose. Remember way back when you and I were real little, how we used to sit under the tree and talk about what we'd change about ourselves if we won a million dollars? You said you'd give all the money to your mother and father if they promised to let you cut your hair. I said I'd change my nose. I'd ask the doctor to get rid of the wide nostrils and fix the tip so that it didn't stick out like it does. But then, later on, I looked at a picture of Mama and realized we had the same nose. Now I know I wouldn't let a doctor come near it, ever. I miss you a lot, Margaret. I know you understand that. Kiss Li'l Jay and Ms. Dell for me. (Not Hattie!)

I read the letter over again before I wrote "Love, Maizon," dotting my *i* with a big circle the way I had done last summer when me and Margaret dug our names into the street the day of Margaret's dad's funeral. That day had been so hard to get through. I folded the letter and put it in an envelope. I was sitting at my desk. Sandy's desk was across the room. I turned and stared at it. Why did I have such a bad feeling all of a sudden? Turning back to my desk again, I took the letter out of its envelope. "P.S." I wrote. "You ever feel scared, Margaret—like something's going to happen to you that's going to change you forever?"

I folded the letter again. But as I licked the envelope and pressed it closed, something inside me froze. What if this letter didn't make any sense to Margaret? What if she thought I was losing my mind here or something? My stomach tightened. Was I the only one who'd ever understand this Blue Hill thing? What it's like to be like this—out of my element is how somebody had described it once—away from everything and everybody that had always been familiar. I held the letter, staring at Margaret's address. Then I added it to the others already piling up in my desk drawer. Maybe one day, I'd show them all to Margaret, and we could sit and read them together. But I wanted to be there with her when she opened each one—I wanted to show her I was okay, that I had survived. That even with all those crazy words on the paper, nothing had changed between us.

Later that night, long after dinner and a quick collect call to Grandma to let her know I was okay, I watched the moon dip behind the main building. In the darkness, the gables glowed blue against the near-black sky. In Brooklyn, I knew, the streetlights would be flickering on now, Ms. Dell would be holding Li'l Jay on her lap, and Hattie and Margaret would be talking quietly on their stoop about everything—and nothing at all.

Chapter Twelve

"It's cool tonight," Sandy whispered into the darkness.

I lay in my bed across from her, feeling strange. I had never shared a room with anyone but Margaret. "Yeah," I said. "It is."

Sandy was shorter than I was, but already she had started growing in places my body didn't even know existed. I had tried not to watch her getting dressed for bed, but couldn't help looking over when she was pulling her T-shirt on. She wasn't flat-chested like me. Her skin was so white I could see the blue veins running along her arms. There was hair under her arms.

"But the air coming in feels nice," I said.

"It does."

We lay silently across from each other for a while and I wondered if Sandy was as aware of my breathing as I was of hers. She breathed in and out slowly. Every now and then, she sighed.

I closed my eyes and tried to imagine Margaret lying across from me. But it didn't work. If it had been Margaret in the room, we would have climbed into the same bed hours ago and now we'd be gossiping and giggling and tickling each other until we cried.

I didn't like sharing with strangers.

"You have brothers and sisters, Maizon?" Sandy asked.

"Nope," I said, annoyed that she had broken through my thoughts. "Just me."

"Sometimes I wish I was an only child. I have two older sisters and two younger brothers," she confided.

"Middle child."

"I guess."

"Are they all in boarding school?"

In the darkness, I could see the shadow of Sandy raising up on her elbow. "Nope, just me. Blue Hill gave me a track scholarship disguised as an academic one."

"I didn't know you were on scholarship. I thought I was the only one."

"Are you kidding? Last year Blue Hill gave out fifty-four academic scholarships. Diana Cortez has one. She's a junior. So do my friends Sonia Chan and Gayle Childs—and Sara Carmona is on scholarship. But they're on different ones than me. Mine isn't for grades. I did lousy in grade school. But I made All-State in the quarter mile *and* I led my softball team to the championships. The paper wrote articles about me. You play sports?"

"Not really."

"You look like you'd be good in basketball. You're so tall and thin."

I felt a flicker of warmth toward Sandy. I had only been called "skinny," never "thin."

"I'm not coordinated. I mean, sometimes I am, but not a lot. Plus, I don't think I'd be good at team sports. I'm sort of an individual."

"That's 'cause you're an only child. My *family* is a team sport. I mean, there're so many of us." Sandy lay back down.

My mind was spinning a little bit. I hadn't even thought that Sandy was on scholarship. I knew I hadn't thought about it because she was white and I just figured that no white people would need help paying for Blue Hill. A long time ago, Ms. Dell had sat me and Margaret down in her kitchen with bowls of her famous Jell-O with cherries in front of us.

"You're gonna learn about racism and death and pain before you're teenagers," she warned. Margaret and I had nodded. By then we knew Ms. Dell had the gift to see into the future. "I'm gonna tell you this," Ms. Dell continued. "Racism doesn't know color, death doesn't know age, and pain doesn't know might."

Lying there, I wondered if it was racist of me to think all white people were rich.

Sandy's breathing slowed. After a while, when I couldn't hear it at all, I knew she was asleep.

I lay awake for a long time. What was it that made white people strange to me, that made Charli and Sheila and Marie seem threatening and safe at the same time? Why hadn't I asked myself these questions before?

"Because you never had to," I heard Ms. Dell murmur somewhere between my waking and sleeping.

Chapter Thirteen

Bells were ringing somewhere far off. Sandy was already dressed and brushing her hair in the mirror when I rubbed my eyes open. The clock beside my bed said six forty-five.

"Good morning, Maizon."

I grumbled something that might have passed for "morning," grabbed my towel and bathrobe, and headed down the hall to the bathroom.

I've never been a morning person and wasn't used to waking up with other people in my room. One thing I liked about being an only child is how much space people give you. Sandy seemed like a nice person, I thought as I let the warm water from the shower run down my neck and back. But to me, nobody's worth talking to at six forty-five in the morning. Other girls hustled in and out of the bathroom. I tried not to watch them through the mirror as I brushed my teeth. They all seemed so comfortable about walking around half-naked in front of other people. Not even Margaret and Grandma had seen me naked since I was small. I wasn't about to start parading what I didn't have in front of strangers.

"You got my side of the room this year," Sandy said, when I came back into the room. "I usually sleep on the side close to the window."

I shrugged and turned toward my dresser to get clean underwear, feeling Sandy's eyes on my back. "If you're slow, you blow," I said. I hadn't meant for it to sound as crabby as it did.

"I like that robe, Maizon. It's pretty."

I slipped on a pair of the new cotton panties Grandma had bought me for school, then draped my robe around my waist and pulled the T-shirt over my head, all the while keeping my back to Sandy. The robe was white with thin green and red stripes running down it. I wasn't used to someone watching me get dressed, and didn't take the robe off until I had pulled on my skirt.

"My grandma bought it for me," I said, draping the robe across the foot of my bed.

"You better hang it up," Sandy warned. "Blue Hill is strict about neatness. If Ms. Bender or Mrs. Miller comes in here and sees it on your bed like that, they're going to say something."

I wanted Sandy to mind her own business. I had every intention of hanging the robe up. When I didn't say anything, Sandy turned back toward the mirror and worked on getting the part straight in the center of her head. She had long brown hair that stopped near her waist, and dark green eyes. Her skin was a little darker than milk. She wasn't pretty. I don't know what it was—her eyes were pretty enough and her hair was beautiful—but it just didn't come together in a way that made her pretty. It made me feel a little sorry for her. People who aren't pretty seem to have a harder time than pretty people. I was lucky. I *knew* I was pretty. I could tell by the way people's faces melted when they met me. The way their eyes sort of softened when I spoke—even if I wasn't saying the nicest things. My grandma always told me how pretty my smile was and how nice my hair looked right after it had been washed, when it was damp and coiling at the nape of my neck and behind my ears. And people were always, always commenting on my eyes, because my lashes are curlier than a lot of people's and my eyes are dark brown—almost black—and slant upward. A lot of people used to tell me I should be a model, especially if I kept growing. Already I was five foot seven. But I had no interest in being a model. I know good and well I'm too smart to waste my intelligence smiling in front of somebody's camera.

"Did you get two pair of socks?" Sandy asked me.

I was sitting on the bed pulling on the white

knee-high socks that went with our uniforms. I nodded.

"A lot of stores sell those same kind," she said. "You can get them almost anywhere."

I stuck my feet into my penny loafers, then checked the clock. It was seven fifteen. Breakfast started at seven thirty and I was supposed to be serving this morning.

"They get upset if you go to class with your uniform wrinkled or dirty," Sandy said. "There's an iron and ironing board in my closet if you ever want to use it."

"Thanks," I said, really meaning it, then held my arm out to check the crease on my blouse. I looked fine.

"See you later, Sandy." I pulled the door closed behind me and ran down the stairs, not wanting to be late on my first full day.

It was warm and bright outside. Grandma had bought me a leather knapsack, and now I slung it across my shoulder and took a deep breath as I made my way across the field. On some trees the leaves had started changing color. Soon, Ms. Bender had told me on the drive here, the trees would be gold and red and burgundy and it would look as though the sky were on fire.

I missed my grandma *so* much and Margaret so much. And besides that, even though everyone was nice to me—or at least, was *trying* to be nice to me, I felt lonely here. Every time I thought of

Madison Street and my friends there, I started trembling and feeling tiny wings banging against my stomach. Every time I thought of home, I wanted to be there.

The dining hall looked bigger with such a few girls in it.

"Maizon!" A girl Susan had introduced me to yesterday, but whose name I couldn't remember, ran up to me. "Miss Norman told me you were thinking about joining the debate team. There's a meeting this afternoon." She tore a piece of paper from her notebook and wrote the information down for me. "It's at four."

Sybil. That was her name. I smiled and took the piece of paper from her. Sybil nodded, as though she had just done her good deed for the day.

Charli came up to me right after Sybil walked away.

"Debate team?" she asked, raising her shades. She had pushed her sleeves up to her elbows and stuck a picture of James Baldwin over the patch of her jacket. I knew she had snuck out of the dorm without anyone seeing her.

I carried a stack of plates to a table near the window, feeling her at my heels. "I'm thinking about it," I said.

"That debate team is *so* corny, Maizon. It's like the nerdiest thing you could do here."

I shrugged and headed back to the kitchen. One of the cooks handed me a plate of toast and a bowl of sliced melon. I carried them back out to the table. Charli was waiting for me.

"And besides," she continued, as though I hadn't interrupted the conversation by leaving, "there are only white girls on the debate team. Don't go turning a Pauli on us."

I rolled my eyes. "There're only five of us in this whole school, Charli. I can't only join the teams where the black girls are. I wouldn't be on anything." I went back to the kitchen for another bowl of melon, set it down at Pauli's table, then came back and sat down across from Charli.

Charli picked up a piece of melon. "Come be on field hockey, girlfriend. Marie and Sheila are on the fencing team."

"Fencing. Now, *that's* corny."

Charli nodded. "I know, but at least they're both on it. We have to stick together, Maizon."

I sat across from her. Two girls we didn't know sat down at our table and smiled. We smiled back, then I let my voice drop to a whisper. "Charli, I'm just gonna check it out. See what they're debating. I might not even join."

"Well," Charli said, grabbing her books and rising, "give it a lot of thought. Some people here make you feel like you shouldn't be here. . . ." She looked at the two girls at our table, who quickly looked away. Charli lowered her voice. "If we want to be strong we have to stick together."

"But you guys are going to be juniors and seniors next year, and where does that leave me?"

Charli shrugged. "Until then, Maizon . . ." she said, grabbing a piece of toast and heading away from the table. "Think about it."

I sighed and folded my arms. The room was loud now; a whole bunch of girls talking at once. I stared across the table, out the window behind it. I want to go home, I thought, feeling the toast go dry in my mouth.

Chapter Fourteen

Mr. Parsons hadn't lied about small classes. There were only twelve girls in my math class, eight in science, eight in French, nine in geography, and fourteen girls in my last class of the day, English. English class met in Laremy Hall, the gabled building I could see from my dorm window. It was right next to the main hall. We sat in a semicircle on the hardwood floor. Our teacher, Mrs. Dexter, wore a poncho and her hair cut short. She sat cross-legged at the opening of the circle. After we had gone around and introduced ourselves, Mrs. Dexter started talking. We would be doing Shakespeare this year, she promised. The class groaned. I hated the little bit of Shakespeare I had read.

"What's all the groaning?" Mrs. Dexter asked, smiling.

The class was silent.

"Can't he get his point across in fewer words?" I asked.

The class laughed. Some girls nodded.

For the next half hour we discussed what we'd be reading—*The Lottery, Animal Farm, A Light in the Forest, A Separate Peace,* and a bunch of other books I hadn't heard of. But other girls in the class seemed to know everything about every book already. I listened to them, embarrassed that I had nothing to contribute, promising myself I'd start in on those books the minute I had a chance.

Then Mrs. Dexter asked us to choose a book we'd like to read in class. Everyone named their favorite book. Mrs. Dexter said some books people suggested were too easy. They got the ax.

"What about you, Maizon?"

I thought for a moment, feeling everyone's eyes on me. "I read a book last summer called *The Bluest Eye,* by a woman named Toni Morrison. I'd want to read that again."

Mrs. Dexter nodded. "That's a marvelous book," she said, and I felt myself grow warm. She wrote our suggestions down on a stray piece of looseleaf paper.

"We're going to start with your suggestions," she said to the class. "Then we'll do *my* reading."

The class groaned again, but underneath the complaining I could feel everybody's excitement, especially my own. I couldn't wait to reread *The Bluest Eye.*

After English, I made my way back to the main hall for the debate meeting. Some of the cross-country team were already doing half-mile sprints on the field. I watched them for a moment, wondering why anyone got a thrill running back and forth. Running only made me tired. Charli rushed by in her field hockey skirt.

"Miss Norman said to tell you to come by tomorrow if you have any interest in playing junior varsity."

I nodded.

"I help her coach them sometimes," Charli called, taking off into a jog. She lifted her shades and winked. "They're *so* cute and tiny," she mocked. I rolled my eyes. I hated being the youngest person, anywhere.

"Hey, Maizon!" Sybil said, opening the door and stepping back to allow me to enter. The room was a corner one, surrounded by windows and covered with dark blue carpeting. The windows let in a lot of sun. There were pictures of explorers on the wall. Chairs were set up in a semicircle the way they had been in all of my classes, except English, where there were no chairs. As I stood in front of one to peel my knapsack from my shoulder, the rest of the girls in the circle stared at me.

"Hi," I said softly, feeling strange. "Hi, everybody."

"Hey, Maizon," different people murmured. I recognized a few of the faces from different classes, but only knew two or three names.

"We've been talking about some of the issues we're going to be debating this year," Sybil said brightly. "But now, I guess, since this is everyone, I hope, we should give our names and stuff before we go on."

I nodded, figuring she was leading the group. "I'm Maizon," I said, nodding toward the circle. "I'm a lower school freshman."

The group murmured a hello and similar introductions followed.

"You're the only freshman, Maizon," Sybil said, after all the introductions had been made.

"I'm used to being the only someone," I said.

The other girls laughed uneasily. I shrugged. The room suddenly felt hot to me and I pulled my collar away from my neck a little and pushed the sleeves of my blouse up to my elbows. Everyone watched this.

"How does it feel?" someone asked me, a girl whose name I didn't remember.

I shrugged again. "I haven't really thought about it much."

"I'd be interested in knowing what it's like here, actually . . ." Sybil said. "I mean, for you."

I said, "I'd be interested in knowing what it's like for *you*."

Sybil gave a quick look around the room and pulled her shoulders to her ears. "I don't think that would be too interesting," she said.

"Why not?"

" 'Cause for me, it's the same as it is for everybody, I guess. Except you and Charli and them," she said.

"How do you know how it is for me?" The room was still. Heads had stopped moving from me to Sybil then back again and had dropped. The others listened without making their listening seem obvious. They were the heart of our conversation, the edges and the middle of it. "I mean, you and I have never even talked to each other, Sybil. That's why I want to know what it's like for you, and then I can see if it's the same for me."

Sybil looked up at me, her small dark eyes moving from one place on my face to another without meeting mine. "You know why it's different for you, Maizon," she said.

"I don't," I said, crossing my legs and leaning toward her. "I *am* smart, but I don't know everything. What makes Blue Hill so different for me?"

Someone coughed. I looked over at her and she covered her mouth with her hand.

I stared hard into Sybil's eyes, all the while knowing that what I was doing was wrong of me. What I saw there was Sybil's own fear of me and this made me madder than I had ever been. She had no right to have such a fear. She had never met me before, had never spoken to me or sat down beside me at dinner. It was the same fear that was in all of their eyes, but Sybil was the bravest. She was in charge and had chosen to raise her eyes and show me the fear there. I hated them all. But because she was brave, I hated Sybil the most.

"What's different?" I asked, giving a quick look around to include the others in this question. "I can't see me now, so you have to tell me, Sybil. What's so *different* about me?"

"You're black, Maizon," Sybil said. There was a near-silent longing in the back of her voice. I heard her desire, if only for a moment, an hour or a day, to be who I am. In Sybil's voice I heard the part of her—of each of them sitting in the room—who had always wanted to be the special one. The one like no other, who stands out and above only because she is allowed to, only because others have chosen to shrink in her presence.

I brushed at my skirt with my hand like I was flicking lint away, but it was really the moment I was ridding myself of. I thought of Marie and how she had brushed her thigh in the same way the first day we met. I was brushing away all of them with a flick of my hand. I felt the room shrink back away from me, felt their individual disappointment and felt the new strength of this power

I had discovered within myself. "Yes, I am," I said, bringing the back of my hand to my eyes as though I were checking for the first time. "I am black, aren't I?"

No one said a word. I listened as someone called the meeting to order. It moved on slowly. I felt the other girls stealing glances at me. I felt mean all of a sudden. As they discussed the coming debates, my skirt had all of my attention. I stared at the dark green pleats riding along the front, at my skinny brown legs beneath it. I raised my feet in front of me and stared at my penny loafers, folded my arms across my chest, exhaled loudly to show my boredom and gazed at the starched, white creases in the sleeves of my blouse.

It seemed like hours before Sybil adjourned the meeting. Only then, with the exits of the others, did the air in the room seem to lift.

"I hope we'll be friends, Maizon," Sybil said, when only she and I were left.

"Yeah. I hope so too." But the lie rode freely on the words, and Sybil knew it.

Chapter Fifteen

"So what's the scoop, dupe?" Charli asked, sitting across from me and blocking my view of the sunset. I had wanted to be alone and had hoped that no one would try to join me for dinner. "To debate or not to debate?"

Marie and Sheila sat down next to us. Two other girls sat at the far end of the table, because all the other tables had already filled up.

"I don't know yet," I said, even though I knew I wouldn't join the debate team.

I turned to Marie and Sheila. "I want to join something. That's the only way I'm going to feel like I belong here."

"You ain't never gonna belong here," Charli said.

"Charli!" Marie scolded.

"You won't ever belong here," Charli corrected herself. "This school isn't about us. It's about them." She gestured toward the two white girls seated at the end of the table. "And them," she said, making a sweep of her arm to include the whole dining room hall.

"Then why are *we* here?" I demanded.

"To get their education, Maizon," Marie said calmly. "To get what they get, small classes, good teachers . . . blah, blah, blah."

"But not to be with them," Sheila added. "There are too few of us."

"You guys don't hang with *any* of them?" I asked.

All three shook their heads.

"I mean," Sheila said, "I speak to some and some of them are cool and everything. But I know I'm not going to make any of those tight friends you grow old with like I've made with Charli and Marie."

"But you don't even give it a chance," I said.

"We gave it a chance, Maizon. We've all been here since we were twelve. I'll be seventeen next May."

I looked at Sheila, but said nothing.

Charli used her knife and fork to cut into her pork chop, then took a bite before she spoke. "The first friend I made here was Elizabeth—she's not here anymore. But me and her were this tight," Charli said, holding up her hand and crossing her middle finger over her index. "We did everything together. Then we went away for summer vacation and I called her. And I swear, the girl acted like she had never heard of me." Charli pressed her hand against the side of her face, and tucked the corner of her lip in, trying to hide her dejection. "It was so messed up. And she wasn't the only one. Lots of girls here are like that."

Sheila touched Charli's shoulder, then looked at me. "When I was in school in Cherryville, people did it to me all the time. They'd be all chummy with me in class. But the minute school was over, it was like 'see ya.' When I heard that Blue Hill was predominantly white, I didn't even want to come here."

"Me either," Charli said.

"But," Sheila continued, "it's not like there are all-black boarding schools anywhere yet. So what's left to do? We come here, find a few black people to hang with, and protect ourselves."

Marie nodded. "It's not even a choice, Maizon. We *want* to protect you because we've seen what could happen to black girls here. It hurts. But you have to make a choice."

"What kind of choice?" I asked, narrowing my eyes. I felt like I was being told what to do—and as I've been told a hundred times, I don't take well to authority.

"Pauli made a choice," Marie said too casually, picking up her roll.

"Well, I'm not Pauli," I said loudly. Some girls turned toward our table. Some snickered.

"Don't embarrass us, Maizon!" Sheila hissed.

"What's wrong with you, anyway? We're just saying we want to protect you."

"I don't need your protection!" I whispered loudly. "I make my own decisions!"

Charli, Marie, and Sheila exchanged looks. Then Marie nodded slightly. This conversation was the end of something. But I wasn't sure what that was.

We ate the rest of our meal in silence.

Chapter Sixteen

Three weeks later, I got another letter from Margaret.

Dear Maizon,

I just want to keep you posted on what's going on here. You still haven't written me. I was thinking maybe you just forgot to. Now I'm thinking you forgot all about me. That's okay. Ms. Dell says you're probably real busy, Maizon, with Blue Hill being such a hard school and all. If you're real busy, don't worry about writing. Best friends don't have to write each other all the time, right? Your grandmother said she got a postcard from you. That was nice that you sent her one. Postcards are nice. I really like them. Li'l Jay is walking around a lot now. Mama says she can't keep him in one place. Sometimes I take him off her hands. Since Daddy died, Mama doesn't have so much patience anymore. Ms. Dell and Hattie and me, we all sit around and talk about you. Did you know that Hattie wrote poetry too? She keeps her poems inside her head. I think maybe you're making a lot of new friends. I hope you don't get a new best friend, Maizon, because I'm not gonna. I hope you remember the promise we made—to be best friends forever and ever. Ms. Dell said sometimes best friends have to go away from each other to find their own way. Then they come back again. I wonder if you'll come back again. I hope you do. I miss you.

Love, Margaret

I folded Margaret's letter up and added it to the small pile of letters inside my drawer. I had taped the poem Margaret sent me to the top of my dresser. The edges were starting to fray and some of the words were fading. Her teacher, Ms. Peazle, had entered the poem in a contest, Margaret wrote to tell me. If it won, Margaret was going to read the poem in front of the mayor. I whispered the poem, feeling the back of my throat closing up with each word:

My pen doesn't write anymore,
It stumbles and trembles in my hand.
If my dad were here—he would understand.
Best of all—it'd be last summer again.

But they've turned off the fire hydrants,
Locked green leaves away.

Sprinkled ashes on you
And sent you on your way.

I wouldn't mind the early autumn
If you came home today.
I'd tell you how much I miss you
And know I'd be okay.

Mama isn't laughing now,
She works hard and she cries.
She wonders when true laughter
Will relieve her of her sighs.
And even when she's smiling,
Her eyes don't smile along.
Her face is growing older,
She doesn't seem as strong.
I worry, 'cause I love her.
Ms. Dell says, "Where there is love,
there is a way."

It's funny how we never know
Exactly how our life will go.
It's funny how a dream can fade
With the break of day.

I'm not sure where you are now,
Though I see you in my dreams
Ms. Dell says the things we see
Are not always as they seem.

So often I'm uncertain
If you have found a new home.
And when I am uncertain
I usually write a poem.

Time can't erase the memory,
and time can't bring you home.
Last summer was a part of me
and now a part is gone.

The poem seemed strange to me all of a sudden. It was about her father and about me all at the same time. I wondered how she had done that—woven two people around and over each other until you couldn't really tell one from the other.

"It's just talent," Ms. Dell would have declared, nodding her head. "That's all it ever is."

Jealousy. It flared up without me even expecting it. I swallowed, but it was still there. Margaret had something I didn't have anymore. A belonging.

Beside her pile of letters, I had one of my own. Letters I had not sent her. I fingered my stack. Some of the envelopes even had stamps on them. For a moment, I thought about mailing one, any one, to let her know I was alive. But I didn't want her to know who I was here, that ever since our conversation at dinner, Charli, Sheila, and Marie hadn't spoken to me, and even though other girls sat down at my table, the only time I talked at mealtime was when Miss Norman or Ms. Bender sat down next to me. I didn't want her to know how alone I was, how even when we made group trips to the movies or dances or state fairs, there was something missing that left me unconnected, feeling like I was on the outside of Blue Hill somehow, watching. Even when people treated me nicely, there was something, always, always, always missing. Something about being here that left me feeling like a shadow, an outline, not whole. So I closed the letter drawer slowly, sat down and began my history homework. I had gotten an *A* on the history quiz.

I looked out the window at the blue hill. The temperature had dropped in the past three weeks and the yard looked cold and empty. Two girls walked across the field wearing the heavy, dark blue jackets with BLUE HILL embroidered across the back in white. Long-dead flowers lay crusting over in abandoned window boxes. In the distance, as Ms. Bender had promised, the leaves on the trees had changed to colors that set the sky on fire.

"Hey, Maizon," Sandy said, slamming into the room. She was on the cross-country and volleyball teams and worked on the school paper and literary magazine. On weekends she usually went home. We didn't see or talk to each other much. When she asked me questions about my life, my answers were guarded. I guess she took this as a sign that I didn't want to be friends with her, and about two weeks into the school year she stopped asking. I liked Sandy. But I was afraid that she'd disappoint me the way Marie and Sheila and Charli had. I didn't want to take chances. I had friends I was sure of back on Madison Street. I'd just have to wait until we were reunited.

"Hey, Sandy," I said, sticking my head further into my book but watching her out of the corner of my eye. Sandy took off her jacket and sweats, then grabbed a towel and headed off to the shower.

I stared out the window until she returned.

"It's getting colder out there," she said. "If you're not used to Connecticut, it could surprise you."

I shrugged, looking at the words in my history book, and said nothing.

"I saw Charli just now. They won their game. She plays basketball too. The team's gonna start practice soon."

"That's nice."

"Are you thinking about playing?"

I shrugged again. "I might give it a try."

"I think you'd be good, Maizon."

"Aren't we *all* good?"

"What d'you mean by that?"

Behind me, I could hear Sandy pulling on pants. It was Saturday and we didn't have to wear our uniforms.

"Nothing."

"You're a hard one to figure out, Maizon." I turned to catch Sandy shaking her head and smiling.

"What do you mean by *that*?" I asked.

"You're hard to get to know. I mean, we're roommates and people are always asking me, 'What's your new roommate like,' and I can't really tell them, because I don't really know."

"They just want to know to be nosy."

"Maybe some of them. But I think there are girls here who wouldn't mind being your friend."

"I have friends. I came here to learn."

"That's the only thing everyone knows about you. That you're smart. My friend Pam is in your math class and she said the teacher asked you to stop raising your hand, because you know all the answers."

"Pam's just jealous. If she studied, she'd know the answers too."

"And my friend Gina has Mrs. Winters's science class with you. She said you know everything there too. They call you teacher's pet."

"Is that what people do, sit around and discuss me?"

"We're just curious, Maizon."

"Well, don't be. I'm not an animal in a zoo."

"Jeez, Maizon," Sandy said, falling back on her bed.

I turned back toward my desk and leaned on my elbows. "I hate this place," I said softly. "I don't belong here."

"Yes, you do." I could hear Sandy walking toward me and brushed my hand quickly over my eye.

"You, Miss Norman, Charli and them, nobody knows what it's like to leave everybody you ever cared about miles and miles behind and come to a place where every single thing you touch or taste or see is unfamiliar to you. This isn't the place for me. I don't want to worry about who I choose to be friends with or where I sit in the cafeteria."

"You shouldn't worry about it," Sandy said, timidly placing her hand on my shoulder.

"But I do worry about it. Marie and Charli and Sheila have been hurt by prejudice and I know I'll get hurt too. I don't want to be the minority. I want to be in a school where that's not an issue. And here, even though nobody really talks about it, it's on everybody's mind. I never had to think about it before and I don't want to think about it now." I sniffed and wiped my nose with the back of my hand.

"Maizon?" Sandy nearly whispered. "Why do you have to think about it all the time?"

I shook my head and brushed her hand away. "You don't understand, Sandy. And I can't explain it to you."

Sandy sighed and walked back to her bed. It felt like there were a million miles between us. But the miles weren't about distance, they were about knowledge and experience and pain.

Chapter Seventeen

"Hi, Grandma," I said cheerfully. It was Sunday morning. I was dressed in my uniform again, because we had to wear them to church. Service would start in a half hour, which gave me some time to talk to Grandma before walking over to the chapel.

"Maizon! Oh, it's so good to hear your voice." Grandma sounded far away. I swallowed. I wanted to see her. "How are you, honey?"

"I'm fine, Grandma. I'm having a fun time here and learning a whole lot. Church is strange though. I've never been in a church full of girls in uniforms."

Grandma laughed.

"It's real different from church with you, Grandma. The sermons are so boring here. And you should see our hymn book. I swear, you'd fall asleep standing!"

"God's there, Maizon," Grandma said. "Don't

fall asleep on His spirit." Grandma chuckled again, which made me blink back tears. "I'm so proud of you. Everyone keeps asking how you're doing."

"Tell everybody I'm doing real good, Grandma. I got an *A* on my history test. And Grandma, guess what?"

I heard Grandma laugh again. "What, my Maizon?"

"Tomorrow, in English, we're going to start discussing *The Bluest Eye.* Remember that book I was reading last summer?"

"That's nice it's on your reading list."

"No, it wasn't. But the teacher took suggestions from everybody and that was my suggestion. So we read it. We discuss *everything* here. It's not like it's only the teacher talking. Everyone in class participates. And Grandma, there're some *smart* girls here!"

"You're one of them, Maizon," Grandma said proudly.

I want to go home, I wanted to shout in the phone. *I don't want to be here.* Bluest Eye *or no* Bluest Eye, *I want to go home!*

"Are you keeping warm, Maizon?"

"Yes, Grandma."

"Are you keeping your hair neat?"

"I always keep it neat. It's grown a little. I might let it grow long."

Grandma chuckled. "And who's going to comb all that hair you're planning to grow?"

I smiled and shut my eyes tightly, trying to picture Grandma standing in the kitchen cradling the phone between her shoulder and ear while she rolled cinnamon-bun dough out on the table. I wondered if Margaret and Li'l Jay were coming over to eat her cinnamon buns and listen to her stories of growing up on a Cheyenne reservation. *Grandma!* I wanted to yell. *Please, Grandma, don't hate me if I come home!*

"I'm happy, Grandma," I said. "Thanks for encouraging me to come here."

"Oh, Maizon," Grandma said again, "I'm so proud of you."

"I'll call you again during the week, if I'm not too busy with schoolwork. How're your legs?"

"They're getting me where I need to go, sweetheart. Don't you worry. And don't interrupt your schoolwork to put in a call to me. I'll be here."

Please be there for me always, Grandma.

I hung up the phone and leaned against the wall, letting my breath out slowly, slowly, slowly. . . .

Chapter Eighteen

"I really like this book, Maizon," one of the girls in my English class said Monday morning. "I'm really glad you suggested it."

I nodded, and found a place in the semicircle.

"Comments!" Mrs. Dexter demanded, when we were all settled.

"I liked it," someone said.

"It was really great. Pecola was so sad."

"Why was she sad?" Mrs. Dexter wanted to know. We didn't have to raise our hand in her class, but if someone else was speaking, we weren't supposed to interrupt.

"She was a black girl who wanted blue eyes," I said. "She figured if she got blue eyes, then everyone would love her."

"That's what's so tragic," the girl sitting closest to Mrs. Dexter said. "I have blue eyes and not everybody loves *me*!"

I rolled my eyes. Mrs. Dexter saw me. "Maizon, you have something to add to that?"

"What was sad, what *is* sad, is that she thought that. And she thought it because the little white girls she saw had blue eyes and happy lives. And it was tragic that she could never be what they were . . . and that she wanted to." I shrugged.

"It is also sad," a blond girl named Annie added, "that ours is a society that teaches us that this is beauty. Pecola took media interpretations as reality. She couldn't see her own beauty."

I blinked. I couldn't believe Annie had caught all this in one reading. I didn't think *any* of the girls in the class would really get what the story was about.

For a moment the rest of the class was silent, as though this were something they had missed. Annie smiled and looked timidly in my direction. I wanted to hug her! She wasn't like the other girls, who saw Pecola as sad for not getting blue eyes. Annie had realized that what was so horrible was that Pecola, a dark-skinned, brown-eyed girl, *wanted* blue eyes.

"Toni Morrison is pretty incredible," someone else offered. "The way she uses children to show us how adults have screwed up society is amazing."

We discussed *The Bluest Eye* for the rest of the class. Slowly, I realized that more and more girls had gotten the story. I wasn't sure how I felt. I wanted them to get it, but at the same time I wanted *The Bluest Eye* to be *my* book—a book only *I*, a black girl from Brooklyn, could interpret. I felt cheated and not as bright as I had felt a few minutes ago.

When class was over, Mrs. Dexter asked me to stay after. "I'm thinking of recommending you for the high school literature course next semester, Maizon," she said. "Do you think you'd like that?"

"I don't know if I'm coming back next semester, Mrs. Dexter," I said carefully. I had not meant to say anything about this and didn't know what had made me tell her.

Mrs. Dexter looked stricken. "Not coming back? Maizon, that's ridiculous. You're doing so well."

I shrugged. "I'm just thinking about it. I'm not a hundred percent sure or anything."

"Well, don't make a rash decision. I'd absolutely hate to lose you."

I swallowed. For some reason, I didn't expect Mrs. Dexter to react with such shock. I knew she liked me but didn't realize how much.

"I'll really, really think about it," I said.

"Is anyone giving you a hard time? Is there anything I could do to keep you here?"

I swallowed and pressed my fingers to my eyes. This was hard.

"I just . . . I just don't want to be here," I

cried. Mrs. Dexter placed her hands on my shoulders. "I don't belong here. . . ."

"Maizon—"

"I don't, Mrs. Dexter. I don't. I don't know where I belong, but it's not here. And I don't know if I'm so mixed-up because I don't know where I'll go after this or because I'm afraid I'll never belong anywhere. I just don't know."

"Oh, Maizon . . ." Mrs. Dexter said, pulling me to her. "I'm sorry," she whispered. "I'm so, so sorry."

"Please don't tell anybody, Mrs. Dexter . . ."

"But Maizon, maybe someone could help you adjust and—"

I pulled away from her and rubbed my eyes. "Please, Mrs. Dexter. Not until I'm sure. Please."

Mrs. Dexter was still for a moment, then she nodded. "You'll come to me before you decide, Maizon?"

"I promise."

"And you'll really give it a lot of thought."

I nodded.

"I'd hate to lose you, Maizon. You're one of the brightest students I've had in a long time."

The schoolwork was harder here. I had spent so many hours buried under the bright light of my desk lamp, studying. In Brooklyn, the work had been easy and I hardly studied at all. But it wasn't any fun to shine here, to get nineties and hundreds on tests. I didn't even care that there were a lot of girls doing better than me here. There sure were a lot doing worse, much worse. But there was a dullness about doing schoolwork here. It didn't matter. I wanted it to matter again like it had at home—in Brooklyn.

I nodded. "I'll tell you when I'm sure, Mrs. Dexter." But I knew, and knew Mrs. Dexter knew, I was lying. I had made up my mind.

Chapter Nineteen

"Hey, Pauli," I yelled, running across the field, my knapsack bumping against my back. I had been at Blue Hill over a month and a half, and somewhere during that time, the fall had been replaced by winter. The wind had an icy edge to it, and too often, the sky was clouded over.

Pauli stopped in the center of the field and turned. When I caught up to her, I saw the confusion in her eyes.

"You called *me*?"

"Yeah," I said, out of breath. Pauli's uniform was blue, with a blue-and-gray plaid blazer over her dark blue skirt. She wore her hair in a pony tail, which she tossed across her shoulder when she spoke. "Where you going?"

Pauli looked at me for a second, then frowned. "I'm going to return a book to Terry, who lives on the third floor of Chapman. Why?"

The ice in her words matched the cold air. I

hadn't expected that. For some reason I thought she'd be interested in walking and talking with me.

"I was wondering. Just wondering," I said, falling into step with her.

"I'm sure Charli and them had a few words to say about me . . . Maizon, right?"

"Yeah."

"Well, whatever they had to say doesn't really matter to me."

"They said I shouldn't stick with you," I offered, feeling only the slightest tinge of guilt for talking behind Charli, Marie, and Sheila's backs.

"Well," Pauli said, pulling her pile of books closer to her chest. "You don't really stick with anybody."

I shrugged. We were walking slowly now. Gusts of cold air cut across my thighs. "I'm trying to decide just where I fit in around here. I feel like I should hang by myself until I get to that point."

Pauli grinned. She had the straightest teeth I had ever seen. "In other words, Charli and them gave you ultimatums and instead of them icing you, you iced them first."

I thought for a moment, then nodded.

"Look, Maizon." Pauli stopped in the center of the field and turned to me. "I don't know what they told you about me being an 'oreo' or whatever they call me. But when I first came here, I wanted to be on the math team really bad, even if it meant that I'd be the only black girl on it. And they gave me ultimatums too. I mean, I respect each of them for their own little thing: Marie is a straight-A student, Sheila is an incredible speaker, and Charli—well, aside from being a great athlete, Charli is just great being Charli. But I had to find my own way here. Everyone on the math team was white and they were all really nice to me. So they were the first girls I became friends with. After that, I made other friends. Let's face it," she said, throwing a hand in the air, "this is a *very* white school. I wasn't about to hang with only three people."

I nodded, because I did get her point . . . almost. "What about the holidays, though, Pauli? What about black history month and kwanza and all those celebrations?"

Pauli rolled her eyes, growing annoyed. "Yeah, well . . . that's kind of hard to explain. I mean, my mom is black and my dad is white. When I was seven they got divorced, and my three brothers and I went to live with my father. We only saw my mother during the summer. Now she's moved to Paris and I only see her for two weeks out of the year. My father didn't make it his business to celebrate any of the holidays with us and what I learned of my black history, I learned in school—an all-white school where my brothers and I were the only ones with black blood running through our veins. We were the 'caramel' kids there, the 'light-bright-near-whites,' the mixed bloods, and every other awful name they could think to call us. First I denied the black part of myself to try to fit, then I denied the white part of me. Then I just accepted both. I mean, I *am* black and white . . . I can't choose between the two."

Pauli was silent for a moment. She looked discouraged all of a sudden, like she had told this story to a hundred different people over the course of her life and not one of them understood.

"I'm ignorant, Maizon. I'll be the first to admit it. In a way I'm like some of the white girls here who want to know all about black people but are afraid to approach them. Charli and them scared me. I didn't want to be told I wasn't 'black enough.' "

"Who decides *that*?" I demanded.

"I feel like some people think they have a right to. I felt like Charli and them felt that way when I wanted to venture out."

"Well, I don't know if I'll stick around here . . ." I said, when we reached the dorm and rushed inside to the warm lobby. "But if I do, I'm going to make my own way too. It would be cool if all of us could be friends—me, you, Charli, Marie, Sheila. . . ."

Pauli nodded, but something in her face told me it could never happen. I never thought about the choices we had to make before. Probably because I never had to make them.

"It's like I'm stuck between two worlds," Pauli said, almost to herself. "And sometimes, neither world is very inviting."

"You think you'll stay at Blue Hill, Pauli?" I asked.

Pauli shrugged. "Where else would I go? Every place is pretty much the same for me."

"What college do you think you'll go to?" It seemed like a long time ago I was sitting in their room listening to Marie and Sheila go back and forth about colleges. Now I wanted to know what Pauli thought.

"Sarah Lawrence," Pauli said firmly. "They have all kinds of girls there. I think I'd be happy in a place like that." She looked at her watch. "I better go. It was nice talking to you, Maizon."

"Nice to talk to you, Pauli."

Pauli climbed halfway up the stairs and leaned over the banister. "I guess I'll see you around, huh?"

I smiled. "Maybe," I said calmly.

Chapter Twenty

"The turkey ran away. Before Thanksgiving day," Sandy sang, slamming her books down on her desk. "They'd said they'd make a *meal* out of him if he should stay! I can't wait!"

"Sandy," I reminded her, "Thanksgiving break is two weeks away!"

"I got the bug, Maizon! I got the serious T-H-A-N-K-S-G-I-V-I-N-G bug. I *can't* wait to get out of here. Why are you studying?"

"Because we have midterms this week and next. I have a history test tomorrow and an English midterm on Thursday."

"Oh." Sandy giggled. We had worked our way toward becoming friends, even playing field hockey together. I hated the skirts. They were worse than our uniforms and twice as short. And the field hockey stick must have been made with Pygmies in mind. After the first practice, I didn't think my back would ever be the same. We had to run up and down a field trying to get this silly ball away from each other. The coach promised me I'd learn the game with practice. But I had absolutely no interest and didn't understand why everyone at Blue Hill had to play a sport. The only good thing about it was that the coach said there was only a very slim chance of me ever starting.

We won our first game two weeks ago—seven-four against Concord. We called them Concord Grape Academy and jumped all over each other when the final whistle blew. I couldn't help noticing that I was the only black person on either team. Nobody else seemed to notice though. The girls on the other team gave us victory high-fives without even blinking. I couldn't help getting the spirit a little bit after we won. The coach took us out for ice cream afterward, and we all crowded around two huge tables, giggling and recounting plays in the game. That night, Sandy and I stayed up late talking sports, coming to the conclusion that she'd be a jock when she grew up and maybe, if I was lucky, I'd learn how to run up and down a hockey field in cleats one day.

Sandy was funny and free-spirited. But there was still a cautious distance between us. Sandy was never sure when I'd get in one of my moods and not speak to her and I was always cautious that she'd get with her friends and pretend she didn't know me. We didn't eat together at school. I had taken to bringing books with me to meals and reading through any conversation someone tried to have with me. I didn't want to chance getting close to anyone. It would just make leaving harder.

"Sandy?" I asked a few minutes later, when she was sitting down at her desk and staring at the cover of her composition book.

"Huh?"

"What do you want to be *if* you grow up?"

Sandy laughed. "An epidemiologist."

"You're going to medical school?"

Sandy shrugged. "Maybe a wife first. Medical school is a lot of money."

"Wifery's a lot of *years*!"

"Nah." Sandy giggled. "A lot of marriages don't last. Then I could collect alimony, which will pay my way through med school. What about you?"

I leaned on my fist and gazed out the window. "I used to want to be a writer. But my friend Margaret aced that. She even won an all-city poetry contest. I don't think that's what I want to be anymore. Now I'm leaning toward being a counselor of some kind. Something where I help people fit in—maybe a shrink."

"A shrink, wow!" Sandy breathed. "I never even thought of that. My mom has a shrink. I never thought of people aspiring to be shrinks. I guess they do, though. That's medical school too."

"School doesn't scare me. . . ."

"Do I know that!"

"A shrink," I said again, almost to myself. "I think I'd like that."

"You'd be good, Maizon," Sandy said. "When you're not crabby, you have a mellow spirit. It's kind of relaxing. Like sometimes, when I come in from a hard workout or a hard class and I see you sitting there studying, and the room is warm and quiet, it just makes me feel good."

"Thanks," I said, really meaning it.

"I'll miss that about you, Maizon," Sandy said softly.

"You haven't told anyone, have you?" One night, after a hockey game, I had sworn Sandy to secrecy, then confessed that I was thinking of leaving Blue Hill.

"I haven't breathed a word. But if I come back from Thanksgiving and see your stuff laid out on the bed, I'll be happy as a nursing kitten."

I smiled and shrugged. "I doubt it. But I'll write you."

"Yeah, sure," Sandy said, cracking her comp book. "That's what they all say."

"You want to take a study break and walk me to the store?"

Sandy slammed her comp book closed as quickly as she had opened it. We pulled our field hockey sweatshirts over our heads and signed out with Ms. Bender, who smiled and nodded knowingly when we said we were taking a walk. A walk, to any Chameleon, meant a trip to Dom's Candy Store.

Sandy and I walked slowly down High Street, hunched into our heavy sweatshirts against the cool air, our hands deep in the pockets. High Street was silent as a stone, the huge houses sitting far back and empty looking, surrounded by the brightly colored trees.

"So much money," Sandy said, almost whispering. She was staring at the houses. Mercedeses and BMWs were parked in front of some of the garages. We passed a house with two small boys playing on the front lawn. They stopped playing when they saw us and stared at me with their mouths kind of opened. I made a face at them, pulling my ears away from my head and crossing my eyes. Sandy laughed. One of the boys smiled a little, but the other looked like he was about to cry. We hurried past them, giggling.

"That's my house!" I said, pointing to a huge three-story house painted white with lavender trimming.

Sandy looked around quickly, then ran a little ahead of me and pointed to a brick house with smoke coming from the chimney and a tire swing in the front yard. "That's mine!" she yelled.

We skipped up the street. "My car, Sandy," I said, when a navy-blue BMW drove past us.

Sandy frowned. "I was going to claim it!"

"If you're slow, you blow."

"I was slew, so I blew." Sandy giggled.

We played my house, my car all the way to Dom's, where Sandy bought two packs of M&Ms and some licorice. Dom must have had a hundred glass jars with every kind of candy you could ever imagine. I wanted to buy a handful of the tiny silver balls, but they hurt my teeth. I walked slowly back and forth, touching one jar after another, while Sandy waited, exaggerating impatience. She tapped her foot and looked up at the ceiling like she would end up in a dead faint or something if I didn't decide soon.

I finally settled on two Hershey Bars, one with almonds and one without and some chocolate kisses.

"You getting your period or something?" Sandy whispered while I was paying.

"What?"

"Whenever my mother is getting her period, she eats like a pound of chocolate."

"God! I hope not! I hope I never get it."

We headed back down High Street.

"Maybe someday I'd like to have it," Sandy said. "You know, just to see what it's like."

"Well, eat your chocolate, Sandy. Maybe then it'll come!"

We laughed, munching as we walked, searching

High Street again for cars and houses we might have missed on our way. There were a lot of beautiful houses. But they weren't on Madison Street.

Sandy started skipping and I followed behind her. She started singing loudly and after she had repeated each verse twice, I picked up the song and started singing along:

Way down South, where bananas grow,
a flea stepped on an elephant's toe.
The elephant cried with tears in his eyes,
"Why don't you pick on someone your own size?"
Ain't it great to be crazy?
Ain't it great to be just like us,
silly and foolish all day long?
Ain't it great to be crazy?

As we skipped along, I realized there was something different about this. The song was different, and so was the place and Sandy. It was "nice" different, even a little fun, even though the emptiness was still there. But this is what Grandma wanted for me, and now I understood. I would keep in touch with Sandy. I wanted to remember her and the few months we shared a room. But I realized I would never tell Margaret about Sandy, even though I'd teach her the song. Sandy would remain a part of me here, of Blue Hill, of sharing with strangers. A part of me that didn't belong to Madison Street anymore or anyone living there.

A farmer had a chicky who wouldn't lay an egg,
so he poured hot water up and down the chicky's
leg.
The chicky cried, the chicky begged,
The chicky laid a hard-boiled egg!
Ain't it great to be crazy . . . ?

Chapter Twenty-one

Two days before Thanksgiving break, Ms. Bender and Miss Norman stopped by. Sandy was at a cross-country meet in another part of Connecticut. I was sitting at my desk, where I had been staring off into nothing, thinking about home for a lot of the afternoon.

"Some quarter, Maizon," Ms. Bender said, sitting at the foot of my bed. Miss Norman sat down on Sandy's bed. "All *A*s."

"Two *A*-pluses," I corrected. "History and English."

They both nodded and smiled. Ms. Bender eyed my suitcase and trunk. Then she looked over and saw my uniform swaying alone in the empty closet.

"You seem to be taking a lot for such a short vacation," Miss Norman said.

"A whole lot," Ms. Bender added.

I stared at the floor. Would they think I had betrayed them?

"You have something to tell us, Maizon?" Miss Norman asked quietly.

"I'm leaving," I said, lifting my head to look at her. "I don't want to come back here."

Miss Norman nodded. "Mrs. Dexter told us you were considering it. We hoped you'd decide not to."

I shook my head. "I don't belong here."

"What will you do?" Ms. Bender asked. I thought about what Charli had told me the first day we met. About Ms. Bender waking up to find her husband had left her. Ms. Bender must have understood emptiness—and the hollowness that replaces the solid places in your life. I looked at her now.

"I'm going to try to find a place where I can fit in being both black and smart. There has to be a place somewhere, right?"

Miss Norman rose and walked over to me, then crouched down so that we were eye-level. "You'll find it, Maizon," she said. She ran her fingers through her hair. "I'm sorry it couldn't be Blue Hill. I was hoping you'd stay."

I shrugged and sniffed. Already my eyes were puffy and red from hours of crying. Not wanting the tears to start up again in front of them, I squeezed my eyes shut for a second until the tears had passed.

"I'm sure you'll find a place for yourself, Maizon. I'm not going to encourage you to stay here, because I can see how unhappy you are, and I can't say I promise you'll be happy if you stay here, because I don't know that."

"I don't want to be a failure," I cried. "Everyone is going to think I'm a failure."

"You have too much . . . too much of everything," Miss Norman said, smiling, "to ever be anybody's failure. Even when you leave here, I know Blue Hill hasn't heard the last of you."

"Have you told your grandmother?" Ms. Bender asked.

I nodded. "My friend Margaret told her for me."

Hattie had answered the phone when I called Ms. Dell's house. For some reason, I had known that was where I'd find Margaret. There was so much static on the phone and I was so scared that I wanted to hang up right then. It seemed like forever before I heard Margaret's voice, sounding tiny and far away. I hadn't realized how much I missed her until I heard her voice through all the static saying "Hello?" Then a whole lot of surprise and relief came into her voice when she said "Maizon?" like she couldn't believe it was me at the other end of the phone. In that quick second, I knew for sure I was not returning to Blue Hill. The way she said my name was my invitation back to Madison Street. Talking to her, I could picture Hattie and Ms. Dell and Li'l Jay in the background, waiting, ready to welcome me home where I belonged.

But still, I lied to Margaret. I told her the girls hated me here, that no one spoke to me. Even with her right there on the phone, I couldn't tell her the truth. All the static got in the way, and the picture of everybody's expectant faces. Even though I knew they'd take me back no matter what, I felt like I needed to give them a good explanation, something really big. But when I heard the way Margaret believed my lies, I started crying, hard. I hadn't wanted to lie to her, but the truth was even harder to tell and I was so afraid she wouldn't understand that it was me who had isolated myself at Blue Hill, that it was me, closing myself off from everyone and everything because I didn't belong to any of it.

I'd have to tell Margaret the truth one day, I knew that. But there was time. Now that I was going home, there'd be lots and lots of time for everything.

"I spoke to Grandma last night too," I said to Ms. Bender and Miss Norman now. "She says to come home and we'll take it from there. She said she doesn't want me to be unhappy. She told me she realizes now that it's too soon for me to be away from her—to be away from home." I swallowed, staring at my fingernails. "Grandma thought Blue Hill was going to be the best thing for me. I used to think my grandma knew everything about what's good and not so good for me. But I think I made her see that I know what's right for me sometimes. Home is. Home's where I should be for now. I mean, there's going to be plenty of time for me to go away. There's college. There's my whole life."

"Then it's settled," Ms. Bender said, rising. "I'll pick you up and get you to the noon train."

I looked up then, feeling relief snatch me up and gently set me down again. This hadn't been so hard after all. It was only the beginning of leaving, but still, I had done it. Almost by myself. And Margaret had been there for me too. Just like she always had.

"I really hate to lose you, Maizon."

Miss Norman rose and patted my shoulder. "I saw you as a point guard . . . starting."

I smiled and wiped my eyes.

"I guess I should say thank you now," I said. "To both of you."

I rose and hugged them both. Miss Norman held me away from her and looked at me a moment. Then she smiled and winked.

"You're going to be fine, Maizon," she promised. "Just fine."

They left and I went back to my desk, leaned on my elbows and stared out the window. I felt like a heavy weight had been lifted off my chest and now I could stumble and float to the next place in my life.

Marie, Charli, and Sheila were walking toward the main hall, arm-in-arm-in-arm as they slip-slided across the now-icy field, wearing thick Blue Hill jackets.

I stared at them. I would miss Charli the most, with her dark shades and easy way. I wondered if Sheila would really go to Spelman and if Marie would change her mind about Ivy League. I wondered if Sandy would forget me or if the girls in my English class would forget Pecola or remember me when they thought of her the way I remembered Margaret's father when I tried to think of my own. I wondered what would happen to Pauli—if she would one day wake up and find herself lost.

"You must have lived another life a long, long time ago," Ms. Dell said to me once. "You're older than your years."

Sitting there, I thought about Ms. Dell's words, and for the first time, they rang true to me. Maybe my gift was that I had lived somewhere a long time before this. Maybe that's where my knowledge came from. Maybe my knowing was my gift the way Ms. Dell's clairvoyance was hers.

I watched the groups of girls walk across the field, bundled up against the cold and the darkening, clouded-over sky. A sadness came over me suddenly. Did I still belong to Madison Street, to

Margaret's stoop and Ms. Dell and Hattie's singing?

When I got home, I'd tell them all about Blue Hill and the leaves turning from green to red and gold. I'd tell them about the rhododendrons, about Charli with her gossip and shades, about how boy-crazy the girls here are. Then maybe I'd tell them about that day at the debate club meeting, about Ms. Bender's husband, about the short walk I took with Pauli across the field. And we'd sit on Margaret's stoop watching it snow, waiting for the Thanksgiving turkey to finish cooking. Then, later on, we'd sit there again, waiting for Christmas, then New Year's to come.

And while we were waiting, I'd get a little sad when I remembered the good times and bad at Blue Hill. But I'd make something of it all . . . something strong and solid. And somewhere inside that strong, solid thing, I'd find a place where smart black girls from Brooklyn could feel like they belonged.

Jacqueline Woodson was born in Ohio and grew up in Greenville, South Carolina, and in Brooklyn. She is the author of *Last Summer with Maizon,* the first book in a trilogy about Margaret and Maizon, which includes *Maizon at Blue Hill.* She has also published a novel for young adults, *The Dear One.*

She has been a fellow at the MacDowell Colony and at the Fine Arts Work Center in Provincetown, Massachusetts.